GERO

INTERNATIONAL BESTSELLING AUTHOR

YD LA MAR

This is a work of fiction. Names, characters, places, and incidents either are the product of the author's imagination or are used fictitiously. Any resemblance to actual persons, living or dead, events, or locales is entirely coincidental.

Copyright © 2023 by YD La Mar

All rights reserved. No part of this book may be reproduced in any form or used in any manner without the written permission of the copyright owner except for the use of quotations in a book review.

Book Cover: YD La Mar
Editor: Jessica Gilly

Acknowledgments

To my wonderful husband, who never bats an eye when I come up with crazy ideas, but instead just adds to it, making my stories come alive. My children, who tell me every day that they are proud of me.

To my beta readers Beth and Gloria. You guys are the real MVP. Thank you for always being down for whatever crazy story I throw your way with no warning. Sabrina, thank you for bouncing ideas off with me!

Mikel, my best friend. I tell you everyday how much you mean to me and my family. The badass leadership crew, you know who you are. You all inspire me everyday to level up, to try harder and to never give up.

To all my readers, thank you for giving me the chance. I hope I can continue to make you guys proud.

Author's Note

It all started with my very first invitation to an anthology. I was ecstatic, I wanted to give it my all, I wanted to punch readers in the face with my writing style and flavor right off the bat.

I think it is safe to say, I did that judging by the feedback I received.

I've been constantly asked if my little short story would be expanded and deep in my heart, *I knew it would*. So here it is, in all its glory. I am happy to report that I love this world.

Forget what you know. I wanted to challenge everyone, as well as myself, on what an omega verse could mean and adapt to.

There will be questions, but I ask that you read it until the end.

I hope you all enjoy GERO as much as I did.

BLURB

In a world strictly divided by social class, I'd grown accustomed to my position.
It was luck that took me from a poor farm boy to a servant in the castle, tending one of the Lord's many Omegas.

Trust me, there are far worse positions than serving a lady in the harem.
As quickly as I came to this position, though, it was taken.

One moment of getting a little too close to the omega I served was enough to land me a prisoner in the dungeons with the others the Lord took favor from.

Kept in cages, tortured or worse for the Lord's pleasure, we're seen as little more than animals.

But I've had enough. I refuse to spend the rest of my life in this filth, doomed to the hands of a Lord not worthy of his station.

My escape isn't going to end in me running to hide.

No... I'm taking my place among the alphas, and the little omega that landed me in this dungeon— she's going to be mine too.

COURTESY WARNING

This book may contain triggers for some. Triggers include but are not limited to non-con, dub-con, violence, choking, degradation, biting, necrophilia, torture, themes of war, kidnapping, urination kink and themes that may be disturbing to some readers.

For the trailblazers.
The ones unafraid to push boundaries.

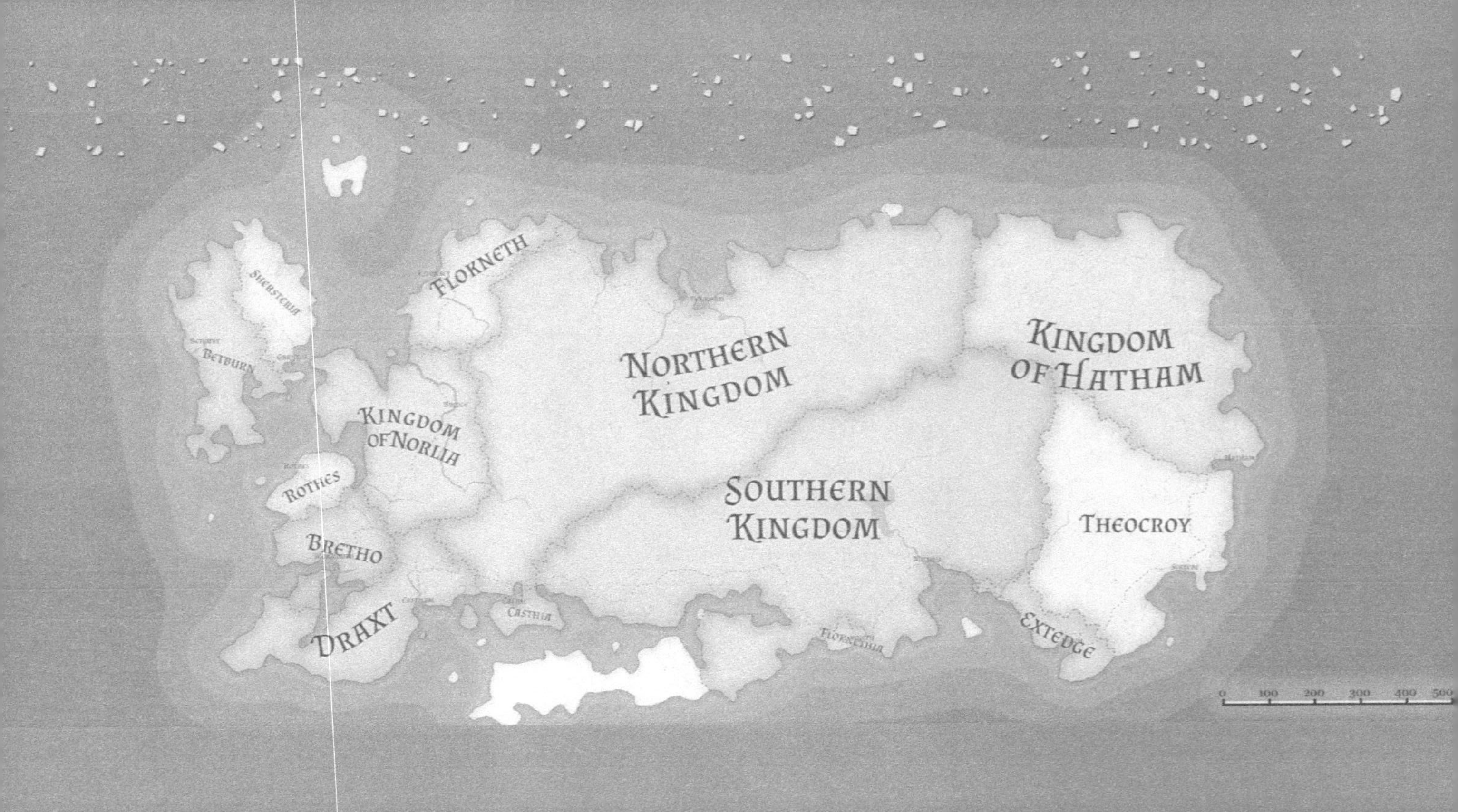

Sherstelia
Betburn
Flokneth
Kingdom of Norlia
Northern Kingdom
Kingdom of Hatham
Rothes
Southern Kingdom
Theocroy
Bretho
Draxt
Casthia
Florentelia
Extedge
0 100 200 300 400 500

I

GERO

The sounds of chains clinking in the darkness fill me with dread. There's a tension in the air, the smell of fear and urine clinging to the walls of the cavern. Heavy footsteps echo, coming closer and closer like a hammering in our skulls. The faint glow of a torchlight casts dancing shadows all around, giving the illusion that demons are taunting us.

A few of the others around me whimper, their bodies shaking and rattling the chains even louder.

"Please, no. No, no, no! Please!"

The torch now sits in its wall handle, the flame dancing higher and higher the longer I stare at it—a trick of the eyes, from being cast in darkness for so long. Despite the pleas coming from one of the prisoners' mouths, the rest of us sit here emotionless, having become used to what goes on down here.

"Did I let you talk, Beta?"

"Please, sir. I-I—" The sound of flesh hitting flesh makes me wince and grit my teeth, preventing me from letting out a sound. I don't want their attention on me. Let Edelgard have his way with whoever else he cast his sights on. It's survival.

Thwack!

"What have I told you about speaking clearly?"

"S-sorry." The sound of his grunts and hacking as he hits the ground with a *thud* puts me on edge. *Alpha is in a mood tonight.*

I recognize the beta's voice. Aenor has been down here long before I was thrown in. We've chatted a few times during the quiet hours. He used to be Alia's servant—the omega mated to Alpha's second.

A growl shakes the bars around us, right before I hear the sound of Aenor being thrown against it followed by a wet slap on the ground. *Blood.*

"You know well to address me correctly, Aenor. Or have you forgotten your place here?" Edelgard's voice has lowered to a different cadence, one he uses right before he makes his claim.

"No, Alpha." *Oh, there's no point in pleading now. Your time is done, my friend.*

The dim glow of the torch allows me to witness Alpha Edelgard's back muscles flexing and heaving as he slowly walks towards Aenor's body, slumped on the ground against the bars. Aenor's cornered like the prey he's made himself to be. The sound of Edelgard's harsh inhales makes the blood drain out of my face in anticipation of what's to come.

As much as we all dislike it, we've been conditioned to expect it.

The others around us start to whimper, the chains

rattling louder. A few further away can be heard grunting and moaning.

I can't look away as Edelgard pulls out his large cock, dripping with precum. Alpha grabs Aenor and forces him on his hands and knees right before he fists his cock and points it at his hole. My own body starts to quake beyond my control with the smell of arousal thickening the air. Edelgard has always had that effect on us all, especially when he's like this. Aenor is starting to come back into a state of wakefulness as Edelgard slams his dick inside of him in one hard thrust, making Aenor howl, the tenor of his voice changing as he screeches in pain.

But Alpha can't be fought. We've all learned that lesson early on. The harder we struggle, the more he takes out on us. No, the best way to survive this life is to submit quickly and live to see another day.

Edelgard sets a brutal pace as his hips pound into Aenor. The sounds of his screams echo off the walls, letting us know he's being torn from the lack of preparation. Liquid splattering on the ground beneath them coupled with the smell of semen makes my mouth water when it shouldn't. I hate the fact that Alpha can control us like this. I hate that he can make us out of our minds, becoming puppets to his needs. Simple, mindless tools. It becomes worse during our cycles, when we beg the guards to put us out of our misery with their cocks.

The grunts continue as Aenor's screams die down into grunts of his own. The blood has probably started to lubricate him by now, easing Alpha's entry. We all become forced audiences to the show in front of us, our eyes like a moth to the only flame cast down here.

"Your pussy feels good, Aenor. Tight, just the way I like it."

Aenor finally comes to his senses. "Yes, Alpha."

"You're going to take all my cum. I can feel my sack tightening with how your pussy is trying to milk me. You enjoy me taking you like this. I'm more than happy to feed it what it needs."

With a growl, Edelgard climaxes, overflowing Aenor's ass and spilling seed all over the ground beneath him. Aenor's knees slip and he hits his head on the bars in front of him with a yelp, making me wince as I continue to sit in the far corner of my cell, stroking my own cock to the smell of sex.

"You've always been a clumsy fool, Aenor." Alpha's knot keeps them attached for the next few minutes. The moment Edelgard pulls his cock out, the splash makes my own cock swell even more as the pleasure within me starts to spike. "Clean that up with your tongue. It's the only meal you'll be getting tonight. The guards will be down in thirty minutes to bring you back to Alia's chambers. She's requested her servant back and I am feeling generous today."

"Yes, Alpha," Aenor let out in a whisper.

"Good boy. See, it isn't so hard for a beta to know his place, is it?" Alpha reminds me of *him*. The memories of my father, staring down at me with blood on his fists, float through my mind.

"Know your place, boy. It isn't that hard."

My dislocated jaw is unable to answer him, so I knew it was coming. Thwack! Another fist to face lands me on the cold hard stone ground right outside our home, in front of the entire village to witness.

Coughing up blood, no one comes to my aid. No one looks my way.

"No, Alpha." The sound of Aenor's voice brings me back to the present.

"Thirty minutes."

Aenor turns on his hands and knees and right before all of us, he bends his head down to lap up everything Edelgard has spilled obediently. The smell of piss becomes stronger, telling me someone's voided during the show, and it makes me come all over my stomach. Sitting here in the darkest corner with my knees up, I bite my lip to stifle the moan that wants to escape.

I'm disgusted with myself for feeling the way I do. I'm disgusted with the fact that Alpha has forced us to become these creatures that live for his attention and for his 'generosity' in letting us back into the kingdom's population whenever he sees fit.

The dim light fades away, taking Alpha's footsteps with it. Slamming the back of my head against the dungeon's walls, I roll it side to side with my eyes closed. The sound of something scraping and the jingle of metal on concrete makes me jerk upright, but the hands on my thighs make me relax and spread my legs open farther.

We've all become animals, forced to live with our instincts as our humanity is slowly stripped away and raped, the way he and the guards do every time they have a need. A tongue laps up my cum as a hand slowly strokes my cock back into its erect state. The rations they give us just barely keep us alive. It's the sex with the others trapped here that keeps us going. We've created a little community within the depths of this hell.

"Yes. Just like that," I growl softly.

As the tongue travels south, I hold my breath. Images of Edelgard's ass flexing make my hips thrust forward and grab the person's hair, shoving my cock deep into his mouth and down his throat. Bernhard has been my cellmate for the past two years. Initially, I was angry at his invasion, but I soon learned to enjoy his presence every night, his hunger for seed giving me a small form of enjoyment as we're left to wither away down here.

"You like sucking my cock, don't you Bernhard? Fuck. Take it all the way down your throat, just like that. So fucking dirty. I bet it was you who pissed earlier, wasn't it? Do you need my cock to make you feel good?"

He nods his head with my dick still in his mouth. I can feel my abs tightening from pleasure, my dick slowly leaking cum as Bernhard sucks harder, trying to get every drop. My mind is wandering to how I'm going to get out of here and slit every guard's throat along my path. The images of bathing the walls in blood make me groan aloud, my fist holding Bernhard's head down until he starts gagging, the squeezing of his throat making me reach the point of no return as I fall over the edge again.

"Fuck, yes! Drink every last drop. You like being my dirty whore, don't you?"

A voice carries from the cell left to ours—Dunstan's. "Fuck, Gero. You're killing me with your dirty talk. I can't take this shit."

"Fuck you, Dunstan. In fact, I'd gladly do it once I get out of here."

I can hear Dunstan pleasuring himself against the bars as he looks across his cell into ours, unashamedly being a voyeur. The wet sound of his dick tells me he's been coming for a while as he listens to us.

Feeling the head of my cock let out one more spurt, I pull Bernhard's head off me and bring him up for a kiss, tasting myself on his lips, imagining it's the lips of an Omega I can call my own someday. When I tire of his entertainment, I get up, rattling my chains, and walk to the other side to be alone.

Sitting down on the opposite corner, I straighten my legs and prepare to rest with my head leaned back against the cell wall.

As if growing up a poor farmer's son wasn't enough, life as a beta has become almost a death sentence. Especially for those who work close to Alpha as servants to his harem of omegas. During their heat, some of us fall back into our animal side, instinct becoming too strong. Any attempt to mount an omega without permission lands us down here. Seems I was lucky and unlucky enough to find my way into the palace as a servant after my father's death.

Finally able to leave my village behind for a better life, I jumped at the opportunity to give my best, climbing up the ranks from cleaning the kitchens to making my way into servitude under one of Alpha's females by the age of forty-two. It was an easy job, the omegas wanting for nothing in their lavish life, as I stood at their beck and call for frivolous things like retrieving snacks from the kitchen at odd hours.

Fuck. I regret the day I caught a whiff of Idalia's heat. I was assigned solely as her beta for the last two years before my imprisonment.

Too late now. These days, my thoughts are filled with planning my escape.

"Get it out of your mind, Gero. It's not going to happen."

Bernhard's voice is soft and pleading, a contrast to his tanned skin and muscular build.

Without opening my eyes, I answered him with full confidence. "If you give up hope, it won't. I'm going to find a way, just you wait and see."

"You're just going to leave me down here?"

"No one is stopping you from coming with me."

"I'd rather stay here where it's safe, and cum with you every night. Is it really so bad?"

He's out of his damn mind, but I understand him. We've all grown to find comfort in the darkness they've exiled us in. But this cannot truly be where it ends for us, not when we have so much more life to live.

"Bernhard, my friend, your perception of life is starting to become askew. Don't lose yourself. Not yet."

"It's really not that bad."

"If you say so." Blocking him out, my mind envisions taking down the guard that feeds us, using his weapon against him, and cutting his head off his shoulders.

The sounds of grunts around me tell me that I'm not the only one affected by our Alpha's visit. The men continue to pleasure themselves, and each other, out of sight. Smiling, I think of the ways I can decapitate heads in my escape from this place, bathing the floors and walls in blood.

Soon, my body relaxes, and I start drifting into the land of crimson dreams.

2

IDALIA

The girls and I are spending our leisure time cross-stitching in the room in silence. Alpha's castle is opulent, each room decorated with the kingdom's crest and colors. Despite the masculinity of the emeralds, my makeshift sisters and I have added our touches to make this particular room ours and ours alone.

Sisters, indeed. As I sit here on the cushioned seat, I stare at the other women with subtle scrutiny. A soft smile graces my face and hides my inward thoughts.

We've all come to terms in our positions as omegas in the Alpha's harem. I have come in third, middle woman to the rest of the girls. It usually means he takes out his anger and emotions on the first two when he comes home from strategy meetings with the other kingdoms. It makes me lucky, I guess. By the time he gets to me, his emotions have already come to heel, a softer male arriving between my legs.

A growl startles us as footsteps come down the adjacent

hallway making all of us perk up attentively. It is a known fact that the soldiers in Edelgard's kingdom are all alphas. A few betas and male omegas serve them when they take their horses out to different locations in order to balance out their energy.

"He hasn't given us any information yet, my Lord," one of the nearby soldiers says.

The sound of another growl and crash makes some of us in the room whimper in fear. What's going on? Is it another brawl?

"Then I will make sure he understands the terms of his stay. Bring him to the dungeons."

"Y-yes, my Lord."

"The rest of you, with me. I have some business to attend to in a week's time in the Northern Kingdom. I will let you know how we plan to arrive. We need to make sure our defenses are up, in case things go awry. You can't trust these Northerners. They'll stab you in the back if they can to expand their kingdom's lands."

"Yes, my Lord," the soldiers respond in unison, their voices fading down the hallway as they continue to walk and talk amongst themselves about the business of men.

"I wonder what's going on between us and the North?" a feminine voice asks beside me.

"Suni, that's not for us to know. You know that. We're omegas. We need to stay in our place." Though I answer her, my eyes are still out the doorway, hoping we can get a glimpse of what might be happening out there.

"But what if our place is being threatened? Don't we have a right to know?"

Annoyed, I look over my shoulder and snap at her.

"That's what the alphas are for—to protect us. We need to trust in them. It's always been the way."

Forcing myself to not curl my lip at her naivety, I resituate myself on the soft chair and put on the pretense of apathy.

Continuing my cross-stitching, I listen to omega number one—Odessa—school omega number five—Suni. Let her calm the young one's fears. I'm not fit for the job. Life has made me cynical and there is no way back from that. Not through finery, not through the cush life in which I've found myself.

The slow motion of pulling needle and thread in and out calms me. I prick my finger on the next pass and I hiss, but not before my pussy clenches. Sticking the finger into my mouth, I suck in the coppery taste and bring my attention back to the girls' conversation.

"Why do you have a servant, and I don't?" *Is there any moment where this one doesn't whine?*

"Because you're the last one in and you don't need one. *Do you?* What do you need a servant for?"

"I don't know; what do *you* use a servant for?" Half of us roll our eyes at her antics.

"Sometimes, Edelgard likes to take out his frustrations from the day. My beta helps me with...necessary aftercare."

"Oh. I wonder if he's done this with me?" Suni innocently asks.

"If you have to wonder, then he hasn't. *Trust me, you'd know.*" Odessa's face winces in emphasis as Suni tilts her head to the side, trying to understand. She really was too young to be brought into the harem.

At fifteen, she came in like all her childhood dreams were

coming true a year ago. She's soft, with fair skin that tells me she's from the Ormsbury region, one of the villages close to the northern border. We were all like her once, disillusioned by the tales of Lord Edelgard, the fiercest alpha in the lands. The stories of how he took down the previous ruler with his bare hands and teeth play in every woman's fantasy, young and old.

The reality of it, though, was a slap in the face. Edelgard is brutal in nature and rules with an iron fist. It's not just with his men, either.

Suni's chirp and curious voice breaks me from my thoughts. "Idalia, how come *you* don't have a servant?"

A dark face and strong jawline flashes before my eyes at the mention. The way his muscles would move, executing whatever command I gave him. I was drunk on power then, and now, I'm without a beta beneath me. Some days I regret it, some days I don't.

"I did," I answer her simply.

I despise the curious sparkle in her eyes. "Oh, what happened? I didn't know you could lose a servant."

"It's a long story."

"Was it nice? Having one, I mean? Now that you don't have one."

I grind my teeth quietly, calming my nerves. She truly is lucky to have come in fifth. She wouldn't be able to handle an alpha at his fullest. He would break her in more ways than one.

"He had his uses." Using him to make Edelgard jealous was a poor plan. I knew it, but in my rage I did it anyway. I should feel bad for getting him removed, but I don't. I was more pissed about the fact that Edelgard chose to ignore me that night despite my attempts at luring him to my bedchambers.

Screams from below echo loudly to the point that the vibrations can be felt along the stone walls of our room, sending chills down my spine. The sound of chains clanking, and growls soften in the distance, but the screams don't stop.

I bite my bottom lip and eagerly listen for more. I need to know what was happening.

"I-I wonder what's happening down there," Suni whispers.

"You shouldn't wonder. Keep your nose out of trouble, Suni."

"Odessa is right. If you know what's good for you, you'll ignore it, like the rest of the people in this place," I reiterate.

The sound of metal hitting stone makes my ear twitch. The guards by the door are either listening to us or fidgeting where they stand, wanting to be where the other men are down below.

Turning to put my cross stitch down on the ground beside the basket of thread, I catch Suni sneaking across the room toward the doorway. I shake my head. Young and stubborn. Not a good combination.

I can hear her trying to ask one of the guards about what's happening when a roar makes the hairs on the back of my neck stand. The rest of us girls snap our gazes to the doorway quickly, but not quick enough to do anything about the blood soaked male who comes barreling through the door. His arms are around the neck of the guard that was talking to Suni, squeezing tightly with a snarl. The gasps behind me are loud. Someone grabs my shoulders, but I can't make myself turn away from the macabre sight in front of me.

Another growl and we all become deaf from Suni's piercing scream. "Ahhhh!"

It's shrill, making me wince but not enough to make me close my eyes. Suni falls to the ground on her ass, but I only see her in my periphery. The brute's muscles start to bulge right before he snaps the neck of the guard with an audible crunch. *Where the hell is the other guard?*

"Ahhhhh!"

In a red flash, the brute is on top of Suni from behind having caught her while she was trying to crawl away towards us, ripping her dress to shreds. My foot takes a step forward, but his voice stops me in my tracks.

"The blood awakens my cock, little one." *Lord Edelgard.*

I didn't recognize him at first. I've never seen him like this, covered in blood with his lightly olive toned skin darkening from the high of his kill. His eyes are fully dilated, his face feral as he clamps his teeth down on her neck, causing her to scream again but this time in pain. The girls behind me have abandoned us, the cool air of their absence letting me know they've retreated further into the heart of the room while I continue to stand and stare.

Suni whimpers, her eyes on me, pleading for some sort of help. *What am I supposed to do?* In fact, I can feel my jealousy rising at being forced to watch Edelgard shove his large leaking cock into her. The smell of their sex intermingling makes my rage rise, and I try not to snarl. I wasn't made to share, but the lot I was given in life is one of an omega, destined to be grouped with others for breeding.

My eyes focus on where his teeth pierce her, red

blooming on her smooth alabaster skin. It tracks down her breasts that are currently bouncing from the force of Edelgard's thrusts. He's finally marked her, and my jealousy starts to intermingle with arousal.

My mouth waters the more he grunts and growls. His arm is wrapped around her chest to prevent her from falling, his lower half continuing to pound away relentlessly. It doesn't prevent the tears leaking out of her eyes—eyes I wish I could scratch out and shove into the vagina that's taking what belongs to me.

The more she sobs, the harder Edelgard rams into her. He's already foregone holding her up, instead opting to push her face into the carpet while he drives himself into her. His ab muscles tighten as my eyes track toward the blood that's coating his shaft. Suni screams in a higher octave when Edelgard buries himself to the hilt, locking his glorious cock inside of her. The sound of his semen splashing onto the carpet makes me want to slice her throat right then and there.

Why am I like this?

Second-hand embarrassment floods me as Suni ugly cries into the floor, her ass still in the air. *Well, she won't have to wonder what Odessa is talking about anymore.* I'm sure she'll even get a servant now.

"Your pussy is tight, milking me. This is where you belong, Omega—beneath me, taking all my cum like the good little girl you are," Alpha purrs, his initial anger having abated now.

Suni is still crying—her second mistake. Our Alpha *hates* to be ignored when he speaks to you.

Edelgard bends over her back and growls into her ear.

"You will speak when spoken to, *female*. I will not tell you again."

"Y-Yes, m-my Lord."

"Your tears are nothing but a waste. It's a good thing your cunt is worth it."

Turning, I slowly walk back to my chair and sit down. I can feel the slick between my legs as I try to find a comfortable position.

Edelgard's head all of a sudden lifts in my direction, his nostrils flaring. Despite garnering his focus, his body is still bent over Suni, making my anger rise. Lifting one of my legs over the arm of the chair, I slowly pull up my long skirt. Edelgard's eyes track my every movement, and I preen at his attention.

When my skirt is all the way up to my waist, Edelgard's nostrils flare again on another harsh inhale. I've been forgoing panties, trying to catch his attention when he's around. It hasn't worked—until *now*.

My fingers travel to my inner thigh, and then to my wet lips, swirling the juices around as they travel up to my clit. Throwing my head back, I dip a finger inside, and then another, thinking about his cock inside of me. Odessa has already been bred and so has Minerva, omega number two. It's Edelgard's fault that I've been left lacking. My special tea to destroy the eggs in my womb has nothing to do with it. He should try harder to fuck me more; then, it wouldn't be a problem.

An audible splash and the smell of Edelgard's cum makes me moan as I stick a third finger inside of myself. My thrusts squelch with every pass, and I bite my lip as my pleasure slowly starts to gather and focus within me. A fist suddenly grabs my hair, snapping my head forward with a jerk. Opening my eyes to look up, I find Edelgard's still erect cock in front of my face, and I open my mouth willingly. The head of his cock is dripping, running down my chin as it passes through my lips, calming the jealousy inside of me. He's so big it makes my jaw ache deliciously. There's a slight metallic taste on top of his natural musk, and it only makes me hotter.

"My little Idalia. Is this what you wanted? Do you have need of my cum inside your willing holes?"

As I moan around his dick, Edelgard starts pushing my head further down until it hits the back of my throat, making me gag. He loves control...and so do I.

"Mmm. I enjoy the way you gag, Idalia. Drink it in, it's all yours. My little cumslut."

I should be upset with the names he calls me—but who am I to argue with the truth?

He comes down my throat and I swallow it all, moaning at his taste—the taste of *mine*. I watch as his hand grips his throbbing knot at the base, his eyes never wavering from mine with each pulse that shoots into my mouth. My throat constricts with every swallow and Alpha pants. Edelgard is going to learn that he belongs to me *just as much* as I belong to him.

Pushing my head down one last time, I gag as he finally pulls out of my mouth and yanks on my legs until my ass is hanging over the edge of the chair's seat, my shoulder blades the only thing remaining on the chair. Trying to hold onto the arms of the chair above my head, Edelgard shoves his cock into my pussy, and I gasp at how much it stretches me. He starts to fuck me slow, and I want to scream and scratch him but my arms continue to be occupied.

He watches the way his cock slides in and out of me, the shaft glistening with our combined juices. I bite my tongue to refrain from saying something I shouldn't. Clenching my pussy around him, I try to urge him faster with body language.

Edelgard chuckles and clucks his tongue at me, making me pout.

"Idalia, you always amuse me so. Is my cock inside of you not enough? You should be happy it's there, giving you pleasure."

"My Lord, you always give me pleasure." The sight of his muscles covered in blood does something to me, too. I've always been one to give into darker sights and pleasures.

"I know. I am a giving male."

Suddenly, he starts plowing into me, hitting me in places that start to edge on pain. Crying out from the roughness of his jostling, I feel like I'm about to fall off the chair when he grows even larger inside of me. Anticipating his end, he surprises me by pulling out, flipping me over, and ramming his dick back inside from behind. The harsh invasion stings, but I moan, urging him on. Urging my husband to take what he needs, and to give me what *I need* in return.

When his dick starts to expand again, his nails dig into the flesh of my hips, causing a sharp sting just as he comes inside of me.

I can't help but cry out, "Yes. *Yes!*"

"You take my cum so well, Idalia. Look at how beautiful you are. Look at how your pussy drinks every last drop. I'll put a babe in you yet, then you'll be happy. I know it's what you've been wanting."

"I just want you, my Lord."

"You have me, Idalia. And my cock. And all the cum you want." His words make me moan as my fingers snake down and start to play with my clit. It's so slippery down there that my fingers fall off the mark a few times, but soon enough, I can feel the pleasure rising higher and higher.

Edelgard growls at being forced to feel everything I give him, since he's knotted inside of me. Pinching my clit and strumming it quickly in circular motions, my pussy clamps down hard on his dick as I cry out in ecstasy.

Edelgard growls against my ear. "Idalia, you're so greedy."

"Only for you."

Thwack! I yelp, the sting on my ass throbbing. His warm hand comes back and soothes the pain as he starts to thrust into me with the little leeway we have thanks to the knot.

The rumors of Edelgard's virility are true—I've never seen a male come so much, even after knotting. My only examples have been watching chambermaids here, and the whores back in my village growing up. The feeling of wetness travels down the inside of my thigh, all the way to my knees.

Edelgard groans when he finally slips out of me, the splash of our combined juices wetting the lower part of my ass, making me moan once more.

"Idalia, come bathe with me. Odessa, Minerva, see that you find a servant for Suni."

"Yes, my Lord," they say in unison.

Taking off my dress and tossing it on the floor, I turn to

walk into Edelgard's arms, uncaring of the blood smearing on my breasts.

"You play with fire, Idalia. I've already killed one guard tonight. Were you wanting me to kill the other by parading naked around him?"

The sound of masculine choking comes from outside the door, but my eyes are still on the man before me.

"Maybe you should find a way to hide my nudity, then, hmm? I have an idea on just h—" I screech when Edelgard picks me up by the ass, lifting me into the air. I wrap my arms around his shoulders and press my chest against him as he kisses me deeply, a hand threading into my hair as he walks us out of the room and into the bathing chambers.

3

GERO

There's an omega down here. *Shit.*

One that's in heat.

Over the years of our torture, they stripped us of our humanity one heat at a time. The entire dungeon is going crazy. My own mind is getting lost in a haze of lust. The smell of his arousal is so strong it stings my nostrils. It also makes me angry—angry that we're subjected to this kind of torture. It's worse than what they do to us down here. I'd take their beatings and their sexual abuses *any day* over this.

The smell of piss hits my nose and I punch the wall beside me. Bernhard has a *thing*—a thing where his arousal is linked to his *fucking bladder*. He tried to explain it to me once, but it didn't make any damn sense. Having been around him long enough, now, it makes *perfect* sense. The relieving feeling he gets from voiding makes his cock hard. Like a small orgasm before the main attraction.

"I can *smell* him from here. It smells so fucking *good.*" Bernhard's voice is strained. He's barely holding on.

"We can all smell his slick. That's the point," I grit out.

"These fucking guards and their mind games."

"*Life* is a fucking mind game."

The sound of footsteps approaches, and we can see two of the guards leisurely coming down the steps. The omega chained in the center of the room looks to be no more than a teenager—twenty years at most. But his slender limbs tell me he's probably a few years younger than that.

"Have you boys had your fun yet?" one of the guards asks aloud.

"What? No 'thank you' for this delicious morsel before you all? How rude of you," the second one chimes in.

The sounds of snarls and growls start to increase around us, some of the prisoners slamming their heads against the bars to try and stop the control the omega has on them. *It won't work.* This is how they were made. This is how we were *all* made. You can't fight nature and instincts at play.

Hiding in the shadows, my tanned skin allows me to blend in more than others as I watch the two guards circle the boy.

"Fuck, you *do* smell good," one of them confesses.

"So...what did you do to land yourself down here, hmm?"

"Must have been something naughty."

"Maybe he'll be willing to play then, if he wants to be naughty."

"N-no, sir. I-I didn't do anything!" The soft lilt of the omega's voice makes my cock leak.

"That's not what we hear."

The taller guard tackles the boy to the ground, his body

landing on top as the omega tries to kick and scream. How he's fighting his instincts, I will never know. The sound of the chains on his ankle starts to clink and ring loudly in my ears, right before other chains start to clink from the prisoners coming closer to the bars to watch the show.

The shorter guard pulls out his cock and starts to stroke it over the other two as he leers at them like a voyeur. The boy uses his size and agility to escape and crawl away, but he's not fast enough. The guard on the ground grabs him by the leg, inadvertently slamming the boy's chin on the concrete beneath him, stunning him long enough for the other guard to get on his knees. Grabbing his hair, the second guard shoves his cock into the boy's mouth right as the first guard shoves his cock into his ass.

They both grunt and growl, but it's drowned out by the snarls coming from all around us. Every last person down here is lost in the lust haze, with the smell of sex rising in the air. We're all becoming rabid. My mind feels heavy, my chest starting to rise and fall faster as my breathing picks up. No matter how much I try to fight it mentally, my own hand finds its way onto my cock, fisting it tightly and stroking it aggressively as I watch the guards breed the boy. *Shit, I bet his ass is tighter than my fist, slick and hot.* The thought makes my abs tighten.

"Is his ass as tight as it looks?"

"Even fucking tighter." The guard's strained voice makes me groan under my breath.

"Shit, I'm going to breed him, too. It won't be hard, since he can't suck for shit, and he keeps sobbing over my cock."

A few more thrusts and the guard in the back groans like he's dying, coming into the boy in spurts, causing the smell of sex to overwhelm the place once more. The air is hot and thick, my breath is picking up, forcing me to inhale through my mouth in an effort to stave off the scent in the air. I can hear Bernhard's own breathing become labored as he comes onto the floor in splashes.

"Fuck! He's tight. That's it, take it all."

The guard in front pulls his dick out and spreads some of his precum all over the boy's face. My mouth waters and my dick start to grow even bigger, telling me I'm close to the edge, the base of my shaft throbbing.

"Stop crying. You know you want this. You're an *omega* —you were made to catch seed and be bred."

"I can't wait to see him growing with a babe. Can you imagine how tight his hole would be then?"

"Fuck, hurry up and pull your dick out. If you keep talking, I'll end up coming too soon."

The guard in front is slowly stroking his cock, his cum leaking every so often. I watch as he takes a finger to swipe the head of his dick and bring it to his mouth, moaning.

"Ulri, hurry the fuck up!" he snarls, a tell-tale sign he's barely holding onto his control just like the rest of us.

With a groan, the guard in the back pulls out, his cum splashing under the boy. The other guard, unable to wait any longer, pushes Ulri to the side, making him fall down as he sticks his cock into the boy's ass.

The boy is quietly sobbing and doesn't move, opting to keep his position with his ass in the air to be used and bred. His submission makes my knot expand in my hand, forcing my climax to come out so quickly I almost become light-headed. Two, three pulses in, and Bernhard's warm mouth clamps over my dick, drinking me down.

I continue to watch the second guard thrust, finally groaning when he knots inside the boy. The omega is so full of cum that the smell of his heat has dissipated, being over-taken by the smell of semen all around us as other prisoners start to service their cell mates in an effort to stave off the madness building within.

"Shit, he is fucking tight, even after your knot," the guard grits out.

"I told you, Vragi."

"Maybe I should ask Alpha if we can keep him as a pet."

"We? We who?"

"You and me. You know damn well this omega is good and bred after catching. Look at our seed leaking out of him. Shit, I'd love to breed him again and again, if he feels *this* good."

"You might be onto something. How are we going to share him, then? We doing a damn schedule or something?"

"Shit, we'll figure it out. Obviously, no one wants him if he's thrown down here with the other rats. If you don't want to share him, Ulri, I'll take him for myself."

"I haven't decided yet. Don't go jumping to conclusions."

Vragi groans as his dick slips out, adding to the cum that's beneath the boy. He bends over and pets the boy like he's a damn dog. The boy doesn't move.

"Would you like that? I'll treat you really good. I'll keep you bred and happy. I can be a good alpha, just you wait and see," the guard placates.

The boy doesn't respond as his body falls to the ground, curling into a fetal position. Both of the guards stand above him, shoulders moving from how hard they're breathing as they stare at him like trade goods to be purchased.

"Alright, you strong-armed me."

Ulri bends down to unlock the shackle and chain on the boy's ankle, then lifts him up in his arms.

I watch as Ulri and Vragi carry him away and up the steps. Pushing Bernhard off me, my back slides against the wall until my ass hits the ground. Bernhard crawls back, suckling on my softened dick. It's another tell-tale sign of his discomfort. Bernhard has a tendency to need to suckle on something to ease whatever is agitating him deeply. This omega being thrown into a den of caged lions has put him on edge, and my scent is the only thing that's helping him find a semblance of calm.

Opening my legs wider, I caress his face as he continues to suckle slowly, his arms wrapping around my waist.

Footsteps nearing us grow louder as a new pair of guards come down to bring our single meal. Pushing Bernhard off me once more, we both stand up and get into position in front of the bars. The rules require us to be where both hands are open and in view, to show that we don't have any weapons on us.

"Alright, ya rats. Who's hungry?"

Mumbles and snarls start up again, but my eyes are too focused on the contents of the tray to care.

"Pipe down! You'll all get your rations in the order you get them."

My muscles tense up, the previous situation still riding high in my bloodstream. In my periphery, I can see some of the prisoners pacing like caged animals, still agitated as well. This is bad timing on their part.

The guard holding the tray reaches the cell beside us first —Philon's and Raban's cell.

"Stop drooling before I decide not to give you your meal," he threatens.

A low growl can be heard in response, but the guard just laughs. Bending down to place the tray on the ground, he straightens back up and uses his booted foot to push the tray the rest of the way into the cell. The scrape of the tray across the concrete makes my head twitch. The sound of a brawl breaks out, a body getting slammed into the bars somewhere nearby.

More mind games. One tray for two prisoners.

The guards chuckle as they walk toward our cell. *I remember this one.* His name is Erling. *Asshole Erling* to most of us here.

He stares at me with a sinister smile as he bends down and places our tray on the ground. Standing back up, I give him a feral smile right back, watching his head tilt to the side in curiosity. When Asshole Erling pushes the tray with his foot, Bernhard grabs his ankle and pulls him to the ground.

Focusing my attention on the remaining male before me, the guard yells something and tries to use his sword to stab Bernhard, but my hand is faster as I grab his, pulling him in and biting down into his flesh until he screams.

As I continue to apply pressure on his arm, his hand opens and the sword clatters to the ground inside our cell. Opening my mouth, I push his sleeve up and bite down again, ripping the flesh with my teeth. I spit the offending matter into his face, making him scream again as he tries to wipe the blood from his eyes. Jumping over Bernhard's prone body still pulling Erling's leg into our cell, I grab the sword and click my teeth.

Remembering our plan, Bernhard's eyes shift to mine

with the signal and roll away right when I bring the sword up over my head, swinging it down with all my weight. It's been a while since I've wielded a weapon and the weight in my hands is comforting. The smell of metal, wet concrete, and blood fill our cell as Erling screams, rolling side to side on the ground, holding his thigh to staunch the wound.

The other guard is so distracted by the detached lower leg that he doesn't see me drive the blade into his chest in one swift move. Clicking my teeth again and Bernhard straightens up and grabs the front of the guard's uniform, impaling him deeper against my blade. His hands are quick as they reach through the bars, patting him down until he finds what we're looking for. The sound of the jingle makes me smile even wider as Bernhard sticks his foot through the bars and pushes the guard's body off the sword, freeing him.

The guard falls right on top of Erling, making him groan in agony. Bernhard quickly moves to the lock and tries all the keys until he finds the one to our cell. The other prisoners have become deathly quiet, everyone collectively holding their breath as they watch the activity happening on our side.

"I got it," Bernhard announces under his breath.

"Good boy. Now let's get out of here."

"I can't believe the plan worked."

"It's been a long time coming."

The sound of the click from the door unlocking makes my heart race and my head feel tight with all that I want to do, all the chaos that will be unleashed. My adrenaline is pumping, heightening my senses beyond the omega's effect on my body earlier. Swinging the metal door open, we both slowly walk out.

Immediately, Bernhard moves toward the other cells to let the rest of the prisoners out while I push the dead guard's body off Erling. When his hand tries to go for his blade, I bring down my own right onto his wrist making him scream like a simpering omega.

The other prisoners are starting to growl and pace, waiting for their turn to get unleashed from their captivity. I can see Bernhard running to the third cell from us to unlock the prison door as I smile at Erling, who bares his teeth at me in a last attempt to not back down.

"Didn't know you like to bottom. After all the times you threated to fuck me, I think you really just want me to fuck *you*," I taunt.

"I'm going to kill you!"

Bending down, I pull the sword out of its scabbard, holding the hilt of both blades in one hand. My mind becomes euphoric at the thoughts of all the carnage to come. I grin down at Erling.

My cock twitches; positions of submission beneath me always seem to do that. Taking a page out of Bernhard's book, I grab my cock and let go. Erling sputters as my piss hits him in the face, basically waterboarding him as he lays there and takes it all.

I groan at the pleasure relieving my bladder gives me. When the stream finally ends, I smile again as I pass one of the blades into my other hand. Slamming both criss crossed on either side of Erling's neck, I jerk both my hands outwards and decapitate him where he lies. The smell of blood overtakes the smell of piss, making some of the freed prisoners standing around me breathe harder. They've basically trained us all to lust after the smell of copper, with everything that happens down here daily.

Growls get louder and louder as the number of freed prisoners starts to increase. Most of us down here are betas, but what Alpha didn't anticipate is the sheer number of agitated males that just had an omega in heat paraded around them.

Bad timing, indeed.

4

IDALIA

Edelgard decided that he wanted me and Frida at the same time—the only two omegas in the harem still not yet with child. I'm sure Suni is by now, from her last encounter—but then again, she hasn't been in heat for a while. She was sobbing in her room for days until Edelgard provided her with a servant of her own. Then it was like nothing happened—one present and she was good as new.

"Idalia, give Frida a chance to suck me."

Sucking hard before I pull my mouth off him, I lick the head of his cock with the flat of my tongue, staring into his eyes. "My Lord, you just taste *so good*. I love the way you feed me."

Edelgard groans and pets my hair. "You're so good to me, Idalia. A perfect omega." *Yet he refuses to mark me the same way he marked Suni.*

"What about me?" Frida's whiney voice grates my ears.

She's just lucky I don't want to do anything to make Edelgard mad at me. She's lucky he hasn't marked her yet either, else I'd be poisoning her food.

"Frida, you can suck all you want. Idalia, get up here and let me taste you." I preen at the command, quickly crawling up his body to sit on his face.

His large hands grip my ass firmly, pulling me towards his mouth as his tongue dives into my already wet folds. Frida must be sucking him, because Edelgard groans against my pussy lips, sending shivers of pleasure down my spine from the vibrations. This is how it should be—Alpha pleasuring *me*, making *me* happy.

There's a commotion outside of our bed chambers and suddenly I'm thrown to the side, bouncing on the bed with a yelp as my body tangles in our sheets. A squeal comes from Frida as she's thrown right beside me, her foot hitting me in the cheek. *The bitch.*

When I finally get untangled, I look up to see Edelgard's naked ass strapping up with weapons. *What is going on?*

"My Lord?"

"Stay here." His voice is stern, taking no arguments.

With quiet and lethal grace, Edelgard exits the room and the sound of growls and metal on metal clashing can be heard in the distance.

"What's happening, Idalia?" Frida whimpers.

"I think there's been a breach. It sounds like fighting inside the walls."

"What should we do?"

"What Edelgard told us to do. Stay here. That's what the guards are for. Let them fight off the threat until it's clear."

"I'm scared," she whispers.

"I can't do anything about that."

The sound of swords clashing gets closer and closer. The once warm room suddenly feels cool. A body is thrown against the wall right outside our door with a loud *thud*, making my heart stop for a second. *It looks like one of the guards!* Another body jumps on top of him, scratching his face off as I watch in horror from the bed. The new male bites down on the guard's neck, blood spurting out of the corner of his mouth and trailing down his own neck.

"Ahhhh!" Startled by Frida's scream beside me, I almost miss the guard that swings his sword down on the new male's back, slicing his spine in one quick movement, spraying blood all over the front of his uniform.

I slap my hand over my mouth to prevent myself from screaming with Frida, who hasn't stopped since she started.

Two more males I don't recognize take down the guard and steal his sword. It's a massacre before our very eyes as the guard manages to take down one of the new males, right before he dies.

The remaining male stands up, naked and soaked in crimson from head to toe, the sword still firmly in his hand. Frida's whimpers catch his attention, and his head snaps our way, his dark blood-soaked locks hanging over his eyes. My eyes widen as he starts running into the room making me jump back onto the bed and head for the other side of the room to create a safe distance.

Frida is paralyzed in place with fear as the male grabs her by the front of her neck and turns her onto her stomach with a single pull. She screams as her body fumbles, but the screams become muffled when the male pushes his forearm into the back of her neck, burying her face into the sheets, suffocating her.

I look left and right, trying to find something I can use as a weapon while the sound of growls and grunts come from in front of me. Dropping to all fours, I start to crawl along the floor. A few paces in, I notice something beneath the bed that's still shaking from the male forcing himself on Frida.

Trying to focus my sights, I see that it's a small scabbard the size of a dagger. Reaching my arms out, I can only touch the tip, but not enough to get a full grasp on it. The male's growls have now turned into groans above me. I can't even hear Frida anymore. Taking a leap of faith on a crazy idea, I turn my body around and use my leg to try and hook the scabbard enough with my foot to bring it closer to me. I'm straining, but it works, and I quickly turn back around to grab it with my hand and bring it out.

The hilt of the dagger glistens with its scattering of emeralds and aquamarines, our Alpha's house colors. Standing back up, I watch in horror as the male climaxes inside of a very limp-looking Frida. His body still slumps over hers, covering a good portion of her very dead body. She must have suffocated during his rutting, not that it seems to matter to him very much, judging by the look of pleasure on his face.

Bad timing on his part.

Pulling the dagger out, I toss the scabbard to the ground and grab the hilt with both hands, bringing it up and swinging it down right into the back of his neck, making him scream. The blood starts to ooze from the wound, making it easy for me to slide the blade back out and slam it down again and again. My mind is watching my movements like it's happening in slow motion, making me think that I need to bring it down harder. My arms become tired with how many times I've stabbed the male. My teeth grit together to the point of making my jaws ache worse than when I've had Edelgard's cock in my mouth.

Breathing heavily, I stare at the two bodies in front of me. The fog in my mind lifts and I finally see the ground meat of his back and neck. The sound of swords still clashing outside brings me back to the present and I grab the sheet from the bed, cutting it with the blood soaked dagger just enough to wrap my naked body like a towel.

Tying a knot near the top of my breast securely, I grab my weapon and slowly exit the room, making sure to keep my ears open in case the fight is closer than I think. I reach the doorway of the bedroom and look left and right a few times before tip-toeing down the hallway. I don't know what the hell is happening, but the males I've seen so far are not dressed like the invasion is coming from outside the kingdom. No, their clothes look dirty and worn. Is this an invasion from one of the surrounding villages? How did they make it so far into this place with all the guards?

Going through secret doors in the wall, I move quickly in a straight path. I have no idea where these hallways lead, as I haven't used them myself, only watching some of the chambermaids using the doors.

"You'll all pay for what you did to us!" a random masculine voice rings out.

"Stand down, Beta. You'll never make it out of here alive."

I don't know how far I've walked but the voices sound like they're coming from just the other side. My fear kicks up and I start to fast walk further along until I see the light of another doorway. Taking a chance since I don't hear anything, I exit the secret hallway to find myself in a room I don't recognize. Omegas aren't allowed to roam too far because of the threats to our safety. Edelgard's omegas are protected even more fiercely than a regular omega.

One step, then another. Being barefoot is an advantage as each quiet step I take lets me move around the room, trying to find the exit. There is a large table in a prominent position in the middle of the room ahead of me that looks to be full of scrolls of some sort. Any other time, I would be nosey and poke around, but right now I need to find Edelgard so he can keep me safe.

Like my thoughts manifest him, a sharp inhale escapes me when Edelgard and another large, dark male break through the wooden door of the room with a crash. They are caught in vicious hand-to-hand combat. I don't know what to do. If I move, I'll catch their attention the way Frida caught the attention of the other male. If I stay, I might be caught in the crossfire anyway.

Remaining as still as I can, my hand grips the dagger's hilt a bit tighter as I watch Edelgard get on top of the dark male and throw fists at his face. Alpha looks even bigger as his muscles bunch and move with every swing. The dark male takes each fist to the face and neck with a feral smile. *Does he not feel anything?* This is such an abnormal response. Alpha gets caught off guard on the next swing when his fist slides against the blood.

The male takes the window of opportunity to grab a large wooden splinter from beside him, shoving it right into Alpha's neck. Edelgard's blood sprays onto his own face. Alpha gurgles, his hand going to the wooden piece that still juts from his throat making me slap my free hand over my mouth as tears form in my eyes.

I'm going to witness something that will scar me forever. My Alpha is down. I'm left open to all threats now. *What do I do?*

The other male knocks Edelgard to the side as he stands over him with a smile full of crimson-coated teeth. His shoulders are wide, much broader than Alpha's from my viewpoint, the muscles rippling with every heaving breath he takes.

Edelgard continues to gurgle but manages to sweep his foot across the ground, knocking the dark male onto his back. With quick reflexes, the male flips back up onto his feet and jumps on top of my Alpha. Two fists to the face, and suddenly the male pushes his thumbs into Edelgard's eyes, finally making me scream.

The sound of the pop and gush of liquid makes me nauseated, but not enough to miss the dark male lift his head in my direction. That crimson smile shows up again, but the exuding menace behind it makes my legs weak.

Taking much too long to make my legs work, I finally turn and run. The sound of the male's heavy footsteps chasing me making me scream once more. *Screw trying to be quiet. I've got a beast hunting me!* He jumps and I duck, making him miss me as I crawl under the table quickly and scramble to get to the other side toward Edelgard's lifeless body.

The sight distracts me for a few seconds too long as the male jumps onto the table with a loud *crash*. He moves suddenly, tackling my body down and inadvertently slamming my head into the concrete floor. My vision blurs, the lights coming in my eyes in a strange, sparkling pattern as my body is jostled around roughly by large, calloused hands.

"Idalia. It seems you've missed me, too."

I whimper. *The voice is so damn familiar.*

His face presses against the back of my neck, the shift in the air telling me he's inhaling my scent. "I've thought about you from the moment they dragged me out of your quarters and into the dungeons below," he purrs.

"G-Gero?" His scent calms me and scares me at the same time.

"So, you *do* remember me." His humorless laugh against my skin sends a shiver down my spine.

A large hand grabs the back of my neck, pushing my face harder into the ground as my ass is lifted into the air. *No, no no no no. I'm not Frida!* Bucking and kicking with all my might, Gero laughs even louder as he grabs my hair firmly and slams my head into the ground with a crunch, stunning me.

The pain radiates through my face, making me groan in misery. Something wet pushes through my vaginal lips, and I know I have no choice but to be at his mercy. He's so much bigger than I am.

"I claim you as *mine,* Omega. Your alpha is dead. Your body belongs to *me* now. I am your new alpha." He's crazy. *You can't change the facts of our hierarchy, can you?* "Whoever says otherwise will die by my hands."

Gero slams into me from behind again and again, his cock just as big as Edelgard's. The stretch makes me whimper and groan from the pain. My nose and forehead are throbbing almost in sync with his thrusts.

"That's it, take my cock. I'm going to breed you, Idalia.

Make you catch my seed. You've teased me too long with this pussy. Isn't this what you wanted?"

I'm unable to say a word, my mind barely able to make complete sentences. The only sounds that escape my lips are gasps and painful groans.

"Fuck, you're tight. Just the way I like it. Going to come all over this pussy and inside of your womb every day just to keep you bred. You're *mine*, Omega." The heat of his body covers my back, scenting me with his musk as he continues to thrust deeply inside of me, hitting my organs with his sheer size.

Another male's voice enters the room. "Gero. I see you've taken care of the problem."

Groaning against the back of my head, Gero doesn't respond to the new male in the room. All he does is lick the perspiration from my skin.

"The smell is killing me. Let me breed her, too." A different male's voice. How many prisoners are there down in the dungeons? What's going to happen to me?

Gero snarls and clicks his teeth against the back of my head, fucking me even harder, as if to make some sort of point. My knees and elbows are getting rug burn with how much he's forcing my body to shift with each deep thrust. My pussy shouldn't be clenching the way it does.

"Raban, tell the others that Edelgard is dead. Tell them Gero is taking his position as Alpha, now," the first newcomer says.

Does that really make me his, then?

"Fuck Bernhard, you're no fucking fun."

"Go, *now!*"

"Shit, I'm going. I'm going."

A few beats of silence pass, the only sounds that can be heard is the squelching of wetness from Gero's cock sliding in and out of my pussy. Why am I so wet?

"I don't trust that beta for a second," the male known as Bernhard mumbles under his breath.

My hair shifts as Gero speaks into the strands with the low timbre of his voice. "I'm going to breed you. Breed you until all you can feel and taste is my cum in all your holes, Idalia. I've waited *so long* for this moment." The cum he speaks of is currently sliding between our bodies, wetting my inner thighs and his hips, marking me.

It must be the cumslut in me, but the sound of his voice in combination with his words makes me slicker, even though my forehead still hurts like a bitch. He groans again and I can feel his cock getting bigger, stretching my vaginal walls to their limit. *Alpha never* got this big. *Shit.*

"You like that, don't you? You're getting wetter—just the way I like it. My little whore, always hungry. I have more than enough to give you, Idalia."

The first spurt of cum that shoots in my womb makes me cry out with unexpected ecstasy. His knot deeply rooted within me holds me captive deliciously. I'm so confused and so aroused all at once.

"That's it. That's a good girl. *Take everything.*"

I can feel my womb filling up to the max with how much he's giving me, my stomach becoming tight with the sheer amount that's already in there.

"Fuck."

I'm lost in the haze of lust, unsure who's cursing. My pussy is starting to pulse and clench with his liquid assault.

"Gero, you smell *so fucking good.* I wish I could drink

down your cum right now but I can't." Bernhard's voice is low and strained.

Gero groans against the back of my head as his nose roots into my hair, inhaling deeply, purring. A new smell enters my mind, confusing me. Is that piss? Another masculine groan and suddenly my body is jostled and pushed forward as Gero snarls like a beast.

"Your pussy is so tight, Gero. My dick is still aching, even though it's inside of you. Can you feel it throbbing?"

"Bernhard, shut up and fuck me if you're going to fuck me." The gravely quality of Gero's voice makes my pussy clench again. *What is wrong with me?* This is the curse of an omega with virile males around. A weakness I both love and hate.

My body is being thrust into each time this Bernhard thrusts into Gero's ass, since his dick is still knotted inside of me.

This strange chain of sex makes me wetter and wetter knowing that Gero is getting fucked by another male while his cock continues to feed cum into my womb.

"Shit, you feel so *good*. I wish I could suck you. I need you to pull out of her so I can drink you down, Gero. *I need it.* I need to taste you so bad." *Why is this so hot?*

Gero bites my shoulder on a particularly hard thrust, making me yelp. My head is still pressed to the ground, each thrust from Bernhard grinding my cheek into the cool concrete beneath me, the edge of the carpet only reaching my forearms. I can feel the cum leaking between my pussy and his knot, flowing down the back of my legs. The smell of sex in the room is suffocating me, reminding me of being in heat while not actually being in one.

Gero groans as his cock finally releases and pushes me flat on the ground, his cum splashing upon his exit.

"Fuck me harder, Bernhard, I need it harder," he grits out.

The masculine grunts and groans make me so aroused that my fingers reach between my legs to play with my clit as I listen to the men fuck each other raw like untamed beasts.

"Gero, please. I need it in my mouth," Bernhard pleads. It's a sound that almost pushes me to the edge.

The men both groan and I turn to look at what's happening behind me, my curiosity getting the better of my senses. My fingers dig into the cum that's still pooled between my legs and run it against my clit, pinching and swirling. I watch with my mouth open as Gero stands up to his full height and Bernhard gets on his knees, his dick still hard and bobbing.

Gero strokes himself roughly, bringing his cock up towards his abs as Bernhard sucks Gero's balls into his mouth with a moan of pleasure, making my pussy clench again at the sight. I can feel my own pleasure quickly rising from the voyeurism, witnessing what looks like an intimate scene between mates. They're so comfortable with each other, this can't be the first time.

"Fuck, yes, that feels good," Gero pants. "You want my cock in your mouth so bad. I'll give it to you. Open up like a good boy."

Bernhard removes Gero's balls from his mouth, remaining on his knees with his mouth open, waiting for his promised offering. I can almost imagine it's me in front of Gero right now. My body tenses up and I cry out in pleasure as I hit the peak of my climax, making my head spin. When my eyelids stop fluttering, I open them to see Gero still stroking his cock in front of Bernhard's open mouth. It must be the lust haze that takes over my body, because suddenly I'm crawling towards Bernhard, and of its own volition, my hand grabs his angry red cock that's beginning to leak all over the floor and starts stroking it for him.

Bernhard's eyes shift to mine only for a second before he brings his attention back to the male in front of him.

Gero growls angrily as he comes all over Bernhard's tongue, his hand firmly holding his exposed knot. After a few pumps, Bernhard wraps his mouth around the head, making me fist his dick harder and harder. My hands are coated with semen as I watch Bernhard's throat continuously swallow.

I don't know where this leaves us, where this leaves me. *Are they going to kill me?* Gero was talking about keeping me to breed. *This must mean I still have purpose, right?*

Wiping my hand on the carpet, I catch sight of my husband's lifeless body right beside us. Guilt slams into me when I realize we've performed all this debauchery right beside him before his body can even get cold. *It wasn't my fault. It wasn't.*

But your body wanting more of Gero's cum and promises of being bred is.

This mind of mine needs to shut her fucking mouth because I don't like the way it's making me feel so conflicted and confused. The same way Gero's scent is making me feel, and Bernhard's, too.

"Idalia, move to the side."

The omega in me automatically follows the strong command without even thinking.

"Bernhard, grab his legs. I'll take his upper half."

"What's the plan here, Gero?"

"We need to make an example out of him in the throne room in front of the kingdom. It's the only way to see our initial plan through."

Bernhard grunts as he lifts one half of Alpha. "What are you planning? I don't remember talking about this part."

"You'll see."

My eyes widen at what they're discussing.

"Idalia, to me." Something inside of me sparks. "Remain by my side."

Looking around quickly, I find the sheet I was using to cover my body and grab it once more, wrapping it tightly around myself. There's more blood on it than I would like, but nothing can be done about it now.

When the men start moving and Gero turns his head away from me, I quickly bend down to grab the dagger that's fallen not too far away from our spot. Holding it behind me, I quicken my steps to catch up with the two men.

5

GERO

The remaining guards that are still alive are thrown into the dungeons and put in chains. *Oh, how the tables have turned in the Southern Kingdom.* My mind continues to plot and plan, making sure we cover our bases with this uprising. The timing of the omega being thrown down there was perfect—it gave us the extra energy and rage we needed to get done what needed to be done.

But my elongated time down in the dungeons below has done something to me. I don't feel the same. I am no longer the man they initially threw down there. I've changed. I think the others have too.

Watching my prison mates and some of the servants toss the last of the dead bodies onto the pile on the grass in front of the palace, my eyes cast around, watching everyone's faces to suss out anyone who may still look loyal to Edelgard.

The problem with the way Edelgard ran things? Only his alphas can serve as guards and soldiers. All the maids and servants are of the beta and omega class, some of them having been mated to said soldiers. He never took into consideration how strong of an influence his betas and omegas had on the soldiers' decisions.

"Alaric, no!" A small, pregnant male breaks from the crowd and runs towards the pile of bodies.

One of the alphas runs after him and picks him up gently, bringing him back into the line. His head bends down as the omega kicks and screams, trying to run back to his mate's body on the pile. Whatever is being said works, because he wraps his arms around the soldier and buries his face into his neck.

The soldiers that stand behind the servants discreetly cast their eyes toward where I stand, and I give them a feral smile.

All my life, others constantly drilled my station into my mind. All my life, I've been told my place in this world. Well, their world is about to turn upside down with the plans I have for the future of this kingdom. The memory of the prior day comes back like the wave of a slowly ebbing orgasm, making my smile grow wider as I continue to stare at the soldiers in front of me.

Tossing his body onto the ground in the throne room, I scan the area, looking at the carnage before me.

"Your Alpha is dead!" I announce.

The fighting and sword clashing slowly stops as everyone around us turns to look in our direction. Idalia is hidden behind the throne, while Bernhard stands firmly beside me.

"Treason!"

"You dare!"

Growls ensue as the betas slice some of the guards and soldiers from behind in their attempt to take me down.

A laugh bubbles out of me like an infection of madness as I lean down to grab Edelgard's hair and pull his head back, stabbing his neck once more. The body has only started to cool slightly, the blood not spraying out as much as I would like since his heart no longer beats, but this will do. Straddling his shoulders, I click my tongue and signal for Bernhard to hold up his body from behind.

My dick gets hard at the sight before me—at the Alpha beneath me. I stick my cock into his new neck wound and groan. I start to fuck it, the muscles within creating a tight and pleasurable cavity for me. I'm glad I didn't slice open his neck.

"By the Gods!" one of Edelgard's alphas cries out.

"He's desecrating our leader!"

Anger grows within me as hot as flames. My face twists into a snarl as I fuck the wound again and again, making sure everyone understands what's happening. Pulling out of him, I grab my knot and watch as my cum spurts all over the gaping hole and Edelgard's slack face, his eyes still open and lifelessly glazed.

"Your leader is no more!" I snap. "His name shall never be spoken here again! I am your leader now!"

The betas all smile and howl, some of them taking the opportunity to bring their blades up behind the soldiers that look like they are still in disbelief of the truth in front of their eyes. Heads are chopped off, limbs hacked as the last of Edelgard's soldiers are taken down in the throne room.

This is my fuck you to the world and their system. We're going to change things, whether the people want it or not. We will no longer be oppressed, pushed down beneath the feet of power-

hungry alphas who use us all as stepping stones to make their lives better.

I look around the room once more at the blood coated faces of my former prison mates. Bernhard stands firm beside me. "Any person who cannot follow the new regime will be killed immediately, per my orders as your new Lord. Follow me and I'll make sure you live to see a new age in the Southern Kingdom. Kingdom Gero."

The freed prisoners and many of the servants cheer en masse as the remaining surrendered soldiers look at each other with uncertainty. They're smart enough to realize that betas and omegas outnumber the alphas in the kingdom. Mass mentality will easily bring them all to their knees.

If they thought Edelgard ruled with an iron fist, they haven't yet met a horde of scorned males with nothing to lose.

The memory soothes me, my mind playing back the sight of Edelgard's mangled body beneath me in the throne room. We hacked his body up and threw it into the pile we are now watching grow.

"The men are ready and awaiting your signal, my Lord." The title makes me smile wider as I flick my head at Bernhard, signaling him while I continue to stand here at attention with my arms crossed.

He nods in response and turns toward the men at the ready with their oils and torches. "Burn them."

Indeed. Burn them all and show everyone what it means to go against the new Alpha. The smoke steadily grows and billows into the sky, clouding everything beneath it. The smell of charred flesh stings all of our nostrils, but no one says a word about it, and no one leaves.

Idalia's soft hands crest over my bicep, stealing my attention and making me look down at her. She's taken to being my omega quickly, reaping all the benefits of my cock inside of her, as well as Bernhard's. Having served under her for a time, I keep my suspicions close to my chest. She thinks she has me fooled, and I let her believe whatever her pretty little head wishes. It keeps her pliant until I figure out what purpose I will have for her in this new kingdom.

Until then, she can warm our beds. She's proven to be a greedy little thing—just what I like in an omega.

"What need do you have of me, little Idalia?" Her sweet scent tingles my nostrils.

"I'm horny." *Of course, she is.*

"You've just had us both this morning." The little omega whimpered and mewled beautifully beneath our invasion.

She pouts, and it makes me chuckle. Conniving little thing she is. Doesn't she know that it's always best to keep your cards to yourself in order to keep the upper hand in the mind games. She's too transparent. It is not the best trait for an omega who wishes to rule by my side.

"You must wait," I tell her. "These duties have to be completed today."

"Yes, my Lord." Her eyes cast downward, but I know this play, too.

I grab the front of her neck and she gasps and looks up at me, her eyes dilating from the rough treatment. The scent of her arousal gets stronger. Bending down, I slam my mouth against hers and push my tongue between her lips, seeking invasion. With a soft moan, she opens up prettily and tangles her tongue with mine. The combination of her scent and taste makes my lust stir. It was something that I wasn't prepared for, no matter how many nights I've imagined it while in the dungeons thinking of revenge.

Once her breathing becomes deeper and her body starts to mold against mine, I push her away and end the kiss. She will have to be satisfied with that. For now.

Without taking my eyes off her, I address my second. "Bernhard, see that the young omega who ran finds a new partner. We need to protect those who are breedable."

"Yes, my Lord."

Idalia submits the longer I stare. Taking my eyes off her, I give Bernhard my full attention. "Inform me of anyone who tries to take what doesn't belong to them. Make sure they know what happens to males who mount before given permission."

The way Bernhard's menacing smile stretches across his face makes my cock twitch. Thoughts of him covered in blood have been playing in my mind lately when Idalia pleasures me with her mouth upon waking.

The smoke and flames grow rapidly towards the sky, taking on a life of their own. The audience has already stepped farther back toward the castle from the heat. It will probably be seen for miles, representing the final culling of the old regime in this kingdom.

Signaling to my men, those that have been promoted to guards, they nod their heads and continue with their duties, making sure the fire doesn't crest *into* the palace. The servants have slowly gone back inside one by one, leaving only a few of the soldiers behind.

Their eyes track me as I make my own way back inside as well, Idalia trailing behind me. The throne room has been fully cleaned by the staff; evidence of what had taken place here only a blip in time now. As I make my way toward the middle of the room, a slight figure runs before me, a beta trailing behind her.

"M-my Lord! Do you h-have need of me? I want to be useful, *please*." The sound of her voice and desperation annoys my ears.

Ignoring her on her knees before me with her head bowed toward the ground, I stare at the beta behind her. He bows once before speaking. "My apologies, Lord Gero. Suni slipped through my grasp and wouldn't be deterred. She was adamant that she needed to speak with you."

A feminine hiss and growl from behind me makes the corner of my lips quirk up for a second. *Always so greedy for my attention.*

I shift my eyes to the bowed figure before me. "And what exactly do you want to be useful for? I already have an omega."

Lifting her head quickly, she stares at me with disbelief. "B-but Ed—I mean, we were previously grouped together for the Lord's pleasure. You haven't visited me. I-I no longer understand my place here."

Pathetic. Her sniveling face makes me lift my lips in a disgusted snarl. *What need do I have of an omega such as this?* I wouldn't want to breed her and continue her weak bloodline. Edelgard was a fool to collect this one in his harem.

"Idalia," I call out.

"Yes, my Lord?" Her voice is on edge, the air scenting subtly with her anger. She is unhappy, and this will not do. These feminine issues grate on my nerves the longer they waste my time.

"What shall I do with this little problem we have?"

Suni's eyes widen in fear as she stands back up and begins to wring her hands in front of her.

This is exactly how they kept us down in the past. They would cast the weak omegas out, while keeping ones like Idalia to breed stronger children. How this one slipped through the crack, I shall never understand. Perhaps Edelgard wanted one he could corrupt and use for entertainment, judging by how young she looks.

The kingdom changes now. These remaining alphas from the previous regime can have the weak while the rest will breed the strong. A dynamic change must happen in order to see the new age come through correctly. My mind is still going over different strategies for change when Idalia's voice catches my full attention.

"I am only an omega. But if you are truly asking me, then I will tell you that I've wanted her dead and gone the moment I met her." Her jealousy thickens the air in the room, making me want to mount her into submission. But I must control my instincts in front of my people; any show of weakness will be used against me.

My hand shoots out and grabs Suni firmly by the neck, her eyes full of alarm and begging for mercy. Dragging her closer, I turn her so her back is against my front, right before I snap her neck with a crunch. Letting her body go, I watch as she lands on the ground unceremoniously in a heap. The beta's mouth hangs open, but he quickly schools his features as he grabs the body by the legs and drags it out towards the front, where I'm sure the flames still burn.

Such a waste. I inhale the subtle smell of the flames and smoke that have reached this room in order to remind me of my mission. "As they say, one must make sure to keep their omega happy in order to keep a happy life. Come, Idalia."

She practically purrs as her arms come around my midsection in an embrace. My nose twitches at the smell of her arousal filling the air, erasing the earlier scent of jealousy and anger. *Insatiable female.* Removing her arms, I continue to walk toward the throne and sit down.

Forbidding Idalia from distracting me from my duties to the kingdom, I signal for her to sit on the smaller throne beside me. She obediently does.

Calling one of the guards that stands to the side against the tapestried wall, I signal for him to inform the staff to begin dinner preparations. The smell of all this cooked human flesh makes my mouth water. Too many years in the dungeons without sufficient food to ease the ache of hunger have maddened me. As the guard bows before his exit, I lean forward in my seat with my elbows resting on my thighs. I'm still thinking through the different possibilities of what can be done here when a court jester enters with noisy flair.

Her body is lithe, her skin sun-kissed. Only her breasts and bottom half is covered as she dances in mesmerizing movements in the center of the room. Her face is painted in a pattern that isn't familiar but entertains the eye as one tries to figure out what her true features are.

Idalia softly growls beside me the longer I stare at the jester, and I swing a warning gaze at her, silencing her immediately.

The sound of staff and servants milling about, bringing out plates and utensils while maneuvering the tables around the room, drowns out my thoughts. Leaning back, I continue to watch the jester as she pulls one of the staff into her antics, making them laugh and dance as well. This is what I wanted the kingdom to become—a place where the once-dubbed low-lives and lower class of society can freely choose to be who they want to be, without the threat of being forced into their supposed *place.*

Bernhard's steps get closer from behind as he brings himself to stand beside me on the right, looking in the same direction. A sigh comes from my left, and I want to rub my hand down my face in agitation. I should remain out here to make an appearance before my people, but it seems my little omega's needs are much too strong to be ignored. Maybe a threat to her position is what she needs to keep herself in line.

"Bernhard, take my place. I'll return shortly. Seems I have another pressing problem I need to handle."

"Yes, my Lord."

"Idalia, to me." Her joyous expression makes me smile, especially with the plan I have in mind. "Jester, your Lord calls. To me."

Idalia's expression falls into confusion, right before it morphs into a frown that she quickly schools. *Oh, little omega, you play with fire.*

When the jester's steps are close enough, I walk out of the room and lead us down the halls and toward the bedchambers we have claimed. Edelgard's old bedchamber is now designated for his bred omegas. The moment their babes are out in the world will be the moment they will be reassigned to other males.

The soft footsteps behind me let me know the females follow without having to give them the command. Good.

Entering the bedchambers, I signal for Idalia to remove her coverings as I begin to remove my own.

The room is spacious with a large bed against the left stone wall covered by the new colors of the kingdom: Red and yellow. No longer is the Southern Kingdom represented by the lion entangled with the wolf. It now holds the crest of a phoenix rising from the ashes.

"Jester, what is your true name?" Standing here naked with my arms crossed, I stare at her face, watching to see what she might be thinking with my command of her in my bedchambers. Inhaling deeply, I try to figure out what I can about the mysterious woman in front of me.

"Cassia, my Lord," she says shyly.

"Your lord requires you to get naked." The smell of Idalia's cunt is already permeating my very being, making my hunger for something else grow.

She smiles demurely and removes the cloth from her breasts first, letting them spill out in their glory. I wonder if she is an omega or a beta? She doesn't smell like an alpha, at least not like any of the alphas here. A hand creeps over my shoulders from behind. Idalia is not one who knows how to share appropriately, an amusing trait for an omega.

Deciding to ignore her, I continue to stare at Cassia as she removes the rest of her clothes. A deep rumbling groan comes out from within my chest when I see that she carries a cock between her legs. I've only seen a few like this back in Caniere, the old village I grew up in. They are cast out and shunned by many, but the time has come for change. By the gods, my imagination runs wild at all the ways we can play when a soft hand grips my rising cock from behind.

The smell of dual arousals from the people in this room

makes my gums ache to bite down on flesh. Controlling my instincts, an idea runs through my head, and my cock twitches in agreement.

"Idalia, get on the bed on your hands and knees. *Now.*"

She quickly complies with enthusiasm, her eyes never leaving my leaking cock. Grabbing Cassia's hand, I drag her towards the bed with me and position her behind Idalia.

I push her hair over her shoulder, lean in and whisper, "Fuck that little omega's hole. Look at how wet she is, how much her hole craves someone to feed it."

"My Lord?" Ignoring Idalia's confused question, I press my body against the female before me, my cock rubbing against her ass.

I stroke Cassia's cock, feeling the wetness on the palms of my hands. Placing a light kiss on the skin of her neck, I firmly grab it and tug it towards Idalia's pussy, forcefully shoving the head inside. Placing my palm on her back, I push Cassia over Idalia's form. My own cock prods her back entrance, avoiding her soaking wet pussy.

"You said you were horny, Idalia. Now take everything Cassia has to give you."

Watching the way Cassia's breasts press against Idalia's back, I thrust forward and breach her tight ring of muscle. She gasps beautifully at my invasion, finally relaxing around me after a few moments, adjusting to my size.

Cassia begins to thrust slowly, making me angry. Pounding into her, I take control of the pace as each one of my thrusts forces Cassia's cock to thrust into Idalia. My abs flex, getting tighter and tighter, my hands grabbing her hips and leaving indentations on her supple skin. Idalia remains quiet as she gets fucked, probably contemplating how she can kill me in my sleep. It makes me laugh internally but doesn't stop what I'm doing.

Pushing both girls onto the bed, I climb up with one knee and roll myself to the side, removing Cassia's cock from Idalia but not removing my own. Idalia gasps in shock and Cassia moans in pleasure. The sheets stick to my skin from my perspiration as my thrusts become more and more erratic. I grab onto her waist while remaining in a seated position and start moving her up and down my dick vigorously, giving me the friction I crave. Growls escape my throat as I slam Cassia down one last time, burying myself inside of her ass, throbbing in her tight hole and making her cry out.

I slide my hands up the front of her body and play with her breasts as I give my omega a command. "Idalia, suck on Cassia's cock. Drink your fill the way I know you've been wanting to all day."

I can already imagine her offended face, but I refuse to give her my attention as I let Cassia go and relax onto the sheets beneath us with my hands clasped behind my head and continue to come into Cassia's ass, filling her up.

The sound of slurps makes my eyes open. Shifting Cassia's body to the side, I watch as her hand grabs the back of Idalia's head and forces it up and down her cock. The sound of her gagging makes my cock twitch when it was just starting to die down.

"Idalia, Idalia, Idalia. My dirty little whore," I chant, sitting up to watch her do what she does best—doing what she's told and taking everything I want her to take.

She moans, and Cassia throws her head back against my shoulder in pleasure from the vibrations of her mouth. Reaching around, I place my hand on top of Cassia's and force Idalia all the way down her shaft. She chokes and suddenly Cassia cries out in ecstasy, her cum running from Idalia's mouth down to my own sack.

My cock, having softened enough, slips out of Cassia's ass as I pull Idalia off the cock in front of her and slam my mouth onto hers, tasting Cassia between us. Our kiss is carnal, desperate. The dueling of the tongues ratchets up the sexual atmosphere around us. Finally, I nip her lip to end the kiss and Idalia yelps.

I grin and stare at her. "Make no mistake, omega—no one breeds you but me and Bernhard. You belong to us, and us alone."

Speaking his name out loud must manifest him because his voice floats from the doorway making my gums ache. "My Lord, dinner is served."

"Cassia, Idalia, get dressed and meet us down in the throne room. I have to speak with Bernhard about important matters."

"Yes, my Lord," they say obediently in unison.

Ignoring my own coverings on the floor, I tilt my head for Bernhard to follow me towards the farther side of the room away from the doorway.

"What is it?"

I wait a few moments after their exit just in case. When their presence is fully gone, I lean into Bernhard and speak under my breath. "I need you to find out where this jester hails from. If she is from one of the surrounding villages."

Curiosity sparkles in his eyes. "Yes, my Lord. Is there anything else I need to know?"

"That's it for now. Let me get dressed and I shall meet you in the throne room for our meal."

6

GERO

"Your antics amuse me, Idalia. But I warn you, you walk a fine line against my fury. Control yourself."

She's been pushing my limits. Ever since our little tryst with the jester, she's been more aggressive. I didn't think it was an omega's trait. Neither is the fact that, over the course of our torture down in the dungeons, something changed within me with every omega in heat they bring down there. Something has changed in Bernhard too, but it's not as evident. I haven't mentioned it to him, and he hasn't brought it up.

Narrowing my eyes in suspicion, I continue to watch her huff about nonsense.

"I just miss him. That's all. Why isn't he here? Where does Bernhard spend all his time?" she bristles.

Leaning my elbow on the chair's armrest, I watch her

and give no answers. It is not her place to know the business of men—especially men who are trying to change a nation.

Bernhard has been sent—as a representative of the new rule—to the closest village with some of the guards and soldiers in order to draft willing individuals into the kingdom's army. With the changing of the guard, we need more loyal followers surrounding us.

"Gero! Are you listening to me?" she whines annoyingly.

I snarl and leap off the chair, landing on top of her and slamming her body into the ground. She's silent. Her eyes widen with fear, but she does not run. Instead, she turns her head slightly to the side and submits to my fury, pacifying the predator within me.

I sniff her neck and graze the tip of my nose against her skin, listening as she takes a shaky sharp inhale.

"Know your place, Omega. Your place is beneath me, not beside me."

Her muscles tense up for a second before she relaxes again.

"Do I make myself clear?"

"Y-Yes, my Lord." The sound of her wavering voice makes me want to mount her, but I won't give her the satisfaction. I've bent to her will too much already since Bernhard's departure.

Despite her pussy keeping me warm, it's just not the same. I shove the thought aside and remove myself from her presence, exiting the room without another word.

Down the hall from our bedchambers, I take a right and head down the steps. The throne room is empty today except for the guards posted in position. They nod their heads in acknowledgement as I walk past them.

What makes a man submit to another for leadership? If not ruled by fear, what makes a man worthy enough to lead the lives of many?

Flashbacks of my past fill me with a deep, slow boiling rage as I head to the armory and scour our cache.

"You, there." The skinny dark haired male cleaning one of the swords looks up. "Do we have an official blacksmith for our weapons?"

"M-My Lord? I am but a servant in the armory. I am unsure."

Useless.

"Find me Raban," I command.

The boy stops his movement but does nothing more.

"Now."

"Y-yes, my Lord!" He jumps up and leaves my sight.

I sigh in resignation at the fact that there needs to be more order. The number of prisoners that followed me are still not enough to take on all the skills and positions necessary to run a kingdom.

Bernhard needs to return quickly.

Grabbing one of the swords off the wooden table, I exit the armory and head outside. The large grassy opening sits just before a small labyrinth made of bushes. Why the elite of society wish to have such a useless thing on their land continues to baffle my mind. I suppose it creates the allure of a wealthy kingdom, to harbor useless things and to let others know that the kingdom is capable of having such items. Avoiding the maze, I head toward the courtyard where some of the men are sparring.

The clanging of metal against metal and the grunts of exertion brings a calm familiarity to my frantic thoughts. I remember sparring as young men back in Caniere. Every village boy's dream was to join Alpha's army.

Little did they know that dreams were worthless. Life threw us where it wanted according to our society's assigned stations.

Anger overflows, coursing through my arms as I suddenly join one of the teams and bring my blade down. The other male blocks my momentum, sending sparks between us through gritted teeth. Shoving me off him, he swings his own blade in my direction, and I lean back far enough for him to miss.

Roars and jeers from the men around us amp up the battle as the remaining male joins in. Two against one, we parry blows and try to knock each other to the ground. None of us are formally trained. Many of us have been brought into the castle as nothing more than servants. I grunt as one of the hits I block digs my heel into the earth. We're going to have to train ourselves for the time being until I can figure out another way without having to go to the old battle master who now sits in our dungeons.

He refused to bow down to the new regime after being given the chance. He chose his path.

I see an opening as my battle partner swings his blade from behind his head. His entire torso is stretched open, and I take that exact moment to utilize my front kick to knock him to the ground. The other battle partner thinks I'm distracted when he swings from his right toward the leg that still holds me up. I jump over the blade and roll on the ground, shooting out my leg to take out his. He cries out in anger as he topples over and lands on his side.

The crowd jeers and hits their shields, wanting more. But

this makeshift battle was enough to get my mind off the past that still plagues me. I grin and extend my hand out to help the two on the ground. They take it willingly with their own smiles.

"Where did you learn to fight dirty like that, Gero?" Cyprian pants.

"What village did you say you were from again?"

I shake my head at their questions. "It matters not where one hails from; it is the life they lead that makes them do what they must to survive."

"You jest, Gero. What can happen in a small village to make one learn skills like that?"

I don't answer Cyprian or Ivo. It is a tale for another time, but not today.

"Men! Continue increasing your skill. We need to be able to defend ourselves from surprise attacks. Who's to say someone hasn't already alerted nearby kingdoms of the fall of Edelgard? We were lucky this time around. We may not be so lucky next time."

The men all mumble their agreement as they take up their battle stances again and continue sparring.

The sun is beginning to fall to the west overhead, indicating that over half the day is gone. Wiping the sweat from my brow, I weigh the sword in my hand. We're going to need to make sure each and every one of us can wield whatever weapons we have in our armory. Swords may not always be available when things go awry.

It was something my father taught me well. The scars on my body are a testament to each and every weapon he used against me. I roll the muscles of my shoulders and walk back toward the armory.

The boy, seeing me, perks up. "My Lord! I did as you commanded! I found Raban."

So eager to please. An omega through and through. How did he end up in the armory, I wonder.

"You did good." Turning my attention to Raban, I address him, "I remember you mentioning once about your grandfather being a blacksmith."

At medium build with dirty blond locks and a beard, Raban's skin has a golden hue. I never inquired about where he hailed from, and he's never been one to supply any more information than he should about himself.

Raban crosses his arms and lifts an eyebrow. "Did I?"

The boy makes himself even smaller as he tries his best to become invisible without removing himself. Raban is another that has been severely affected by our time in the dungeons. Or perhaps, he's always been this way and I just didn't know it.

"Yes. If I remember correctly, it was during one of your lonelier nights with Philon." I leave the rest for interpretation. The boy doesn't need to hear about the life we led in the dungeons.

Raban curls his lip before responding. "Well, *my Lord*, you would be correct. My grandfather came from a long line of blacksmiths until spirits got the best of my father, making him a drunkard."

I remember this story whispered in the darkness as well. His grandfather disowned his son, therefore disowning his entire family, after a bad quarrel. Raban lived life as a rogue and thief in order to keep food on the table for his mother and siblings while his father drank his life away, leaving twelve-year-old Raban to take up position as the man of the house.

How he found himself in the Edelgard's dungeons remains a mystery.

"We need someone assigned to the armory. We need to fashion more weapons as we wait for Bernhard to recruit more men for our kingdom."

"And you truly think that person should be me? A rogue?" Raban throws his head back and laughs at the absurdity of what I'm asking. He claps his hands behind his head and cocks his head at me.

My serious expression doesn't falter, and his smile slowly turns into a scowl.

"In situations like these, it is not our qualifications that get us where we need to be. It is necessity that puts us there. In order to strengthen the kingdom *we* chose to conquer, we need to address all of our possible weaknesses."

Raban stares at me for a moment, his mind full of thoughts he chooses not to vocalize. I can see him grinding his teeth and tightening his jaw.

"Don't blame me if they're unbalanced. That's all on you." Raban turns to the boy and snaps, "Get the forge going. It's going to be long days ahead."

THE SERVANTS SIT DOWN WITH THE MEN AS THEY TAKE THEIR dinners. The smell of pheasant and pork roast fill the air, cloaking it with false comforts.

I stand from my chair and signal for everyone to keep enjoying their meal as I exit the room and walk beyond the outer halls toward one of the windows that face the courtyard. The night brings with it a chill, but it doesn't phase me one bit. Cold nights in the dungeons were plenty.

Soft footsteps behind me make my hairs stand on end as I quickly turn around to find Idalia standing a few feet away. She's grown to learn my moods and adjusts all her actions accordingly. I'm unsure how I feel about that simple fact.

"I wanted to accompany you, my Lord," she whispers, sights cast lower on my face rather than my eyes.

I lean back against the stone wall, crossing my arms and ankles in a relaxed pose. "Are you sure you didn't want to accompany anyone else? There are plenty of men who need their beds warmed."

Her eyes sharpen, but she doesn't look me in the eye. I push her. I need to test her. To see if she really is what she says she is—devoted to the new king. Why should she be? I killed her alpha in front of her. I took her only security in this world and then forcefully claimed her as my own.

She still hasn't poisoned me, and I have yet to wake up with a missing eye. What game does she play?

"I am your omega."

It can't be that simple.

"Why?"

She jumps at my quick response. I prod her, curious at what her answer might be.

"Why are you my omega? What makes you so special?"

Her lips tremble, though her eyes fan with embers. "Y-you claimed me. You said I was yours."

I straighten to my full height and walk toward her. She remains in place until we're toe to toe. "So I did."

Idalia is a small thing, standing to my chest with a beautiful dark mane that curls at the ends when she lets it down. Her curves would bring any virile male to aggression, but it's her personality that leaves me perplexed.

She's aggressive and possessive for an omega. But the same could be said about me, a beta who leads. Is this why I find myself attracted to her even though some days I want to cast her off to others?

I grip her chin and force her eyes up. The moment her eyes lock with mine is the moment I search for the answer.

Fire. Lust. Ambition. Greed. So many swirling emotions that I cannot pinpoint what goes on in that pretty little head of hers. She grasps my wrists gently and brings my thumb into her mouth, sucking it and swirling the pad of my finger with her tongue suggestively.

I growl.

"Do I not please you, my Lord?" she says breathlessly. I should fuck her and send her on her way. It's what she followed me for, isn't it?

"Is that what you hope to do?"

She nods and rubs her cheek against the palm of my hand. With her head tilted, the light of the moon outside the window casts a subtle glow against her skin. I stare at her unmarred neck.

"Horses at the gate!" someone cries out.

The announcement breaks me from my thoughts. I turn to walk back toward the window and peer in the direction some of my men are beginning to run toward. No one seems in distress, so I assume the visitor is a welcomed one.

One of the riders jumps off the horse while it's still moving and walks the rest of the way. It's his cadence that sends goosebumps on my skin. My hands grip the windowsill right before I turn and head out the palace to greet our returning men.

Bernhard sees me and grins. We give each other a companionable embrace the moment we meet, slapping each other on the back.

"I see your trip was fruitful," I tell him, noticing the new additions to the small band of men that was initially sent out.

"It wasn't hard to convince the people of the injustices the previous system has put upon our lives. Everyone wants to see change. Everyone wants to witness the kingdom rise under the rule of a beta whose name has already been whispered among the young men as a legend."

I let out a hearty laugh at that, pulling Bernhard toward the castle as everyone greets each other.

"Philon, lead the new men to their quarters. They will be staying with the servants for now until we can decide where they should be distributed." Bernhard gives the command like it's something he's done all his life. Pride swells in my chest at having him by my side. "What's with that stupid grin on your face, Gero? Did you miss me?"

I wrap my arm around his neck and let him struggle for a few moments before shoving him off me. He laughs and crows like a lunatic, annoying me.

"Idalia missed your cock and I had to make sure it came home intact."

"Is that what she told you? She has two cocks, what does

she desperately need mine for? It hasn't been that long. Is your old age catching up with you? Hard to get it up?"

My fist flies, but Bernhard ducks and wraps his arm around my neck, pulling me against his chest.

"I've missed your cock in my mouth. I've hungered for you the entire trip home," he whispers against my ear.

I groan and shove him off me, walking the rest of the way alone, hoping the cold night air would keep my lust abated until the day's duties are done.

It's her squeal that makes me wince. Idalia runs toward us and flings herself into Bernhard's arms, kissing him unabashedly in front of all our new guests.

Some of the new men look at us both questioningly back and forth with hints of judgment. Society looks down on triads like ours, still stuck in the ways of the past with their harems for the elite and monogamy for the poor. The men who have shared the dungeons with us shove them toward the other building, informing them of what they are to expect in the coming days.

Bernhard's hand is hidden between them as their mouths make love. A spark of something ignites within me but I ignore it. The job of a king is never done. And today, we must make sure that the new recruits understand that all they have been taught are moot. Socioeconomic class and social designations have no place here. Everything they've learned will be put into question as they train under the new command. Everyone will be made to earn their keep through skill and skill alone.

Cutting their activity short, I speak up. "Idalia, save it for the bedroom. I require Bernhard for matters of the kingdom."

"Would it be so bad to have a quick reunion? I've missed him so much."

I snarl, and just as I'm about to rip her away from Bernhard, he removes her from his body, then turns her and pats her on the ass before I can get there. "Run along. Your king has ordered you to leave."

She huffs and peeks at me under her lashes but does what she's told. I'm going to have to watch my temper around her in times like these.

"Seems you've left her bed empty to be *this* angry. Your balls are too full."

Ignoring his jab, I ask, "How far did you travel?"

Bernhard knows I'm changing the subject, so he grins and doesn't mention it. We walk past the throne room and head toward the study. Though a separate space from the battle room, it is still used for planning between the small group of men I trust.

"To Bannackburn."

I look at him surprised. "That far?"

From my memory, the villagers from my hometown say Bannackburn is over a hundred miles west from there.

Grabbing one of the maps, I unravel the scroll and lay it on the table in the center of the room. Edelgard's blood still stains the stone beneath our feet. The servants were unable to completely remove him, instead simply pulling the rug over the evidence of what happened here.

Bernhard comes to stand beside me and looks at the map. He points his finger just before the southeastern corner of the Southern Kingdom. I am impressed. Pride swells in my chest once more at how fast he must have pushed the men he had with him on this mission.

I stand there with my chin on my hand, staring at the different villages that surround the kingdom when I feel his arm come around my waist.

"I didn't want to be away from you that long. It was a good thing the group was small. By the time we made our way back through the route we went down, villagers were gathered waiting to join us on the trip back to the castle." Bernhard rubs his nose against my arm and any thoughts of strategy went out the window as my dick received all the necessary blood my head needed.

When his hand drifts towards my backside, I let out a growl and pin him face down against the table with my forearm against the back of his neck, my body bent over his and my dick nestled between his cheeks.

"It took you long enough to get back to me," I snap. My aggression is getting the best of me, and Bernhard is going to get the brunt of my anger.

"Fuck, Gero. I need you like this. I needed this."

I rip his pants down his legs, trapping them together. Gripping his exposed flesh, I massage and mold it forcefully until his skin pinkens under my palm. Bernhard is panting on the table, one of his hands wrapped around his dick, stroking.

Idalia could never understand what it is like between Bernhard and I. She never had to experience it, never had to go through what we did. She never had to forge a bond so deep that the other person has become the other half of your soul.

Quickly unfastening my own pants, I stroke my cock until there's enough precum to lubricate the crown. Bernhard growls as I line myself up and breach the tight ring of muscle and invade his body. Our time in the dungeons has made us used to rough and raw treatment. We've come to seek it now.

His muscles tighten on the next slow thrust, making me grit my teeth. Time and time again, I try to break free from everything we've known, but it isn't working. It isn't what I need—what we both need. *Enough teasing*. Leaning over him further, I viciously begin pounding out my frustration and he takes everything I give him.

The desk moves with each of my thrusts, and I wrap my arms around his hip, forcing his hand off his cock, replacing it with my own. With a strong grip, I clamp down behind the crown of his head, preventing him from voiding onto the ground like he wants to.

He groans at the torture but doesn't stop me, instead encouraging me as he backs up his body against mine with each countermove.

Our tryst is hot and heavy, quick and passionate. The air around us is thick with sexual tension. On a final thrust, I bury myself inside of him deeply, spilling and knotting, connecting us for the next few moments. My mind swirls with both lust and confusion at the changes in my body. I can't remember when I started knotting...

"Fuck, Gero. Please."

I stroke and squeeze his head one last time before releasing my grip and pointing his dick toward the ground beneath the table. Bernhard moans as he lets go and the smell of piss threatens to overtake the smell of sex.

The sound of something shifting makes my head snap to the side only to find no one there. *Do we have spies?* It could be any of the newcomers, the servant's quarters are on the other side of the castle. Suddenly, my mood sours and in the next few moments my dick slips out of Bernhard, my release coating his skin.

Tucking myself back in, I reroll the map, placing it back where it belongs and leave the room without another word. My guard is up with every step I take and every room I pass. My eyes scan the area, but I do not find anything disturbed.

When I reach the throne room, I see that everyone has finished their evening meal and have already cleaned up for the night. Turning around, I make my way back to the study only to hear a familiar feminine voice.

"Bernhard…"

He doesn't respond but the sound of copulation is loud as flesh hits flesh vigorously. I step into the room to find Idalia bent over where Bernhard once was. I watch as Bernhard's ass muscles flex with each thrust and slowly walk around the table to the other side.

Idalia's face is full of ecstasy, her eyes closed and unaware of my presence, lost in her lust. Bernhard stares into my eyes with a sly grin on his face as he pulls out, spilling onto her back.

She growls like a ferocious little kitten but stops the moment she realizes where his gaze lands. Comically, her mouth forms an "o" without making another sound.

"If you're done, I'd like to retire for the night before I have to get back to matters of the kingdom."

7

IDALIA

"Do you have any primrose oil and licorice root?"

The servant in the kitchen startles at my question, not noticing me behind her as she quietly stirs the stew. With her hand over her chest, she turns and takes a deep dramatic breath.

"My apologies! I didn't even hear you over the boiling. What were you asking for, again?"

"It's okay. I shouldn't be down here anyway, but I was wondering if you have any primrose oil and licorice root in the pantry?"

"Oh, perhaps. The younger maids find lots of things when they're out picking berries and such. Let me turn the heat down on this stew pot and help you look."

I peek left and right under my lashes and make sure no one is around close enough to hear our conversation.

We both walk past a few servants, saying our hellos until we finally reach the room in the back designated for dry ingredients. It is an open doorway without an actual door. While the maid busily starts looking at labels over the glass jars, my eyes scan the shelves on the bottom. I've snuck in here a time or two during Edelgard's reign to prevent him from breeding me. Today, though, I'm here for a whole other reason.

My eyes catch half the word, the bottle having turned partially to the back. *Shatav* is all I see, but it's what I need.

"Hmm, let me look on this side so you don't have to look alone," I offer. She doesn't turn around, so I quickly squat down and remove some of the ingredients and shove them inside the secret pocket I've sewn into my dress.

Standing back up, I come to her side pretending to help once more as she says, "Ah ha! There they are."

She hands me some of the ingredients, and I curtsey a thank you before leaving her smiling face. Most of the servants in the kitchen are omegas, always willing to help when they see another omega in their midst.

"If you need anything else..."

I'm already headed out through the kitchens with minimal greetings to the other servants.

Quickly running back up to the main level, I enter my private bedchambers and go towards the back by the window. There's a loose stone that covers some of my other ingredients hidden inside the wall.

Looking left and right for a few moments, I make sure the door is closed and no one is here before I focus back on my task. Gero hasn't assigned any of the ladies to be in waiting for me, but you never know what decisions are made when the men are out doing whatever they do.

Grabbing the wooden box, I open it up and drop the

primrose seed and licorice into the cup. Taking the herb root out of my pocket, I place it inside the small mortar and begin grinding it. Scraping the powder into my cup, I look for the yellow flowers I picked the other day when Gero was busy meeting his men about business matters. With everything in place, I stand to grab my water basin from this morning. I was able to save some fresh water after pouring what I needed to cleanse myself into another bowl I stole from the kitchen some time ago.

Pouring the remnants of what I have left into the cup, I use the spoon stored away in the box to start stirring. When the water begins to change color, I chug the entire contents down quickly, avoiding the particles at the bottom. The sound of men's voices drift through my bedroom window and my heart rate kicks up. Tossing all the evidence quickly back into the box haphazardly, I shove everything behind the wall and replace the stone as best as I can.

The voices are receding, but I'm still on edge at almost getting caught. Wiping the sweat off my brow, I start to take off my outer layer to cool down. I pace the room and fiddle with random items just in case someone walks by and knocks on my door. After a few moments, an ache forms in my stomach and my brow starts to perspire. Fanning myself, I cease my pretend fiddling and look about the room. The sight of my cool sheets calls to me like a siren. Quickly making my way to the bed, I crawl beneath them and groan. The voices around the palace drift in and out of my aware-ness, the same way my mind does.

"Mmm," I whimper.

I try to tamp down the ache, but it only churns harder within me with each passing moment. My body is getting so hot I don't want to touch my own skin. My limbs feel like they're moving through water—slow and hard to control, under an invisible pressure. I must have drifted off a little because suddenly I'm jerking awake at the sound of men sparring not far away.

Are they inside my room? I didn't hear anyone enter. No, that doesn't make any sense. They must be outside my bedroom window. I rub my face on the sheets with my eyes closed, my ears straining to listen to everything around me and trying to decipher what's real and what's not. The men call to each other, yelling commands and techniques. I flutter my eyes open—or at least attempt to with no success. My eyelids feel heavy, and my body still feels like it's burning up.

Why am I burning up?

My mouth is so dry it forces me to crawl off the bed and look for my water basin. When I get there, there's only a couple of gulps left, but it will have to do. Lifting the basin, some of the water splashes down the side of my lips, giving my skin a small reprieve from the internal torture.

"Fuck. What a waste," I mumble.

Crawling back to bed, I try to find a comfortable position. The increased wetness between my legs agitates me, especially when there's nothing to soothe that particular ache. After what feels like twenty minutes of shuffling, nothing I do is good enough. Pushing the pillows here and there, I use the sheets to bunch up and rearrange them around me.

It's not enough. It just doesn't feel right.

I need to find a cool spot, but none of it is cool enough for my burning skin. Laying my head down, the perspiration sticks to the silken sheets and my face slides across it. Ugh, it's barely doing anything at all. I shuffle the blankets once more and make another attempt, but my body burns up, making the sheets quickly warm and uncomfortable once again.

"It's the clothes. The clothes," I chant.

My limbs shake as I fight the layers of clothing I have on in an effort to remove them, in an effort to feel more of the cool air against my skin. Some of the fabric rips but I pay it no mind. I need them off me! The moment my skin comes into contact with the room's air, my sigh of relief almost turns into a moan of ecstasy. My nipples harden and I roll onto my stomach to try and add a little bit of friction against them.

Sudden growls make goosebumps rise on my skin as I snap my head to the doorway, my hair a mess and tickling where it lands. I barely register what's happening when a large, dark figure jumps on top of me and starts forcefully rooting against my neck. His body is fire hot, but for some reason, it doesn't matter, because right now my breasts feel heavy and tender, and they love the way his chest is rubbing against them.

I push his head where I want him to go—south—and Gero clamps his mouth over my nipple and sucks hard, scraping his teeth against my flesh and making me cry out. His dick is already wet and seeking my entrance as he kisses a trail along the underside of my breast and back upwards toward the crook of my neck. I can feel myself gushing, my slick out of my control, wetting the inside of my thighs as Gero groans and slides right into my pussy with one hard thrust.

"Idalia. You smell so good," he groans against my neck, and I sigh.

"Gero. I need you to fuck me so badly," I plead. I want him more than I've ever wanted him. My mind is buzzing and lost in a haze of lust that only revolves around him filling my womb with his virile seed. *Please. Please, Gero!*

"I know," he whispers in a raw voice. "I'll give you what you need. Open up for me wider so I can fuck you deeper."

The sound of a skirmish outside my open bedroom door makes Gero growl. Suddenly, his mouth clamps down on the crook of my neck, piercing my skin making me scream in both pain and pleasure. Slowly the feeling of euphoria overtakes me with every seductive suck. Lost in a new sort of subspace, it sounds like another fight breaks out outside my bedchambers, but I can only concentrate on how good his cock feels inside of me at the moment.

The only semblance of clarity I can grasp onto is the simple fact that Gero has marked me as his, passionately and irrevocably. The sheets beneath us become wetter and wetter as the smell of sex invades my every thought and pore. I want to be bred. I need to be bred. I need him to ravish me.

A new voice makes me whimper. *"Leave us, now!"*

Bernhard's command is loud and clear, making my eyes snap open to look over Gero's shoulders that continue to bunch as he thrust into me, again and again, grinding himself as deep as he can go. My tongue runs along his shoulder, tasting his sweat as my eyes track Bernhard's every movement toward us. Possessiveness makes my gums ache as my tongue continues to tease Gero, keeping him in place.

Bernhard slams the door closed, making my breath stutter as I watch him place a beam on the large metal hinges on either side to lock everyone out.

"Idalia, your heat is driving all the males mad," he accuses in a deliciously guttural voice. Bernhard walks towards me, divesting his sparring gear with every step, leaving them haphazardly on the floor of my bedroom. "Do you know how many of our own men Gero and I had to stab to get here first?"

A smile breaks on my face as I watch Bernhard's cock slap his abs when he finally divests his pants. *It's their fault, really.* After that stint with Cassia and Bernhard's return, both the men have been pissing me off with their lack of attention to me when I really need it. Don't they realize that sex a couple of times a day just isn't enough for me?

They'll learn now.

The concoction my great grandmother used to help the village women got her burned at the stake under Edelgard's regime. It was the first time he set his sights on me, the glow of the fire fresh on my youthful skin, and it was the last time I saw my family.

Images of flames, burnt skin, and screams of agony dissipate into nothingness as the feel of Gero's cock pounding into me pulls me back to the present. The smell of his masculine musk makes me delirious with greed.

"Idalia, you smell so..." Bernhard groans as he fists his cock aggressively watching us both entwined in limbs.

Suddenly he turns around, walks back to the closed door, slams his hand and forehead against the wall, groaning aloud like a man in pain. The smell of urine hits my nose, but it only spurs on my lust. Gero doesn't stop his grinding, both of us understanding Bernhard and his needs, both of us clawing at each other to bury his dick deeper inside of my womb.

Bernhard sounds absolutely feral as he turns back around. "Fuck!"

Gero groans, rolling onto his back and pulling me with him. He grabs my hips and moves my body like a rag doll as he sees fit. It makes me feel dainty. It makes me crave this desperation I'm finally seeing and feeling from him.

All of a sudden, Bernhard's body is behind me, growling possessively behind my neck as he roots his nose into my hair. His sharp inhales send goosebumps across my skin. In the next moment, he pushes my body harder against Gero, who bares his blood coated teeth at him in warning.

I shouldn't get excited over this, but I am.

A forearm pushes me down, keeping me in place, as another wet cock prods my back entrance. My mind is clouded over with the smell of cum reaching my nose. Both of these men have their unique scents, both of them overly masculine that makes me mewl in submission. My mouth is hungry, latching onto Gero's chest with my teeth lightly, licking up his sweat, wanting more of him inside of me. Wanting more of everything inside of me.

"Fuck, you're so tight around my cock," Gero groans, grabbing the back of my head and forcing me to lick more of him and he continues to deeply grind into my pussy.

"She's about to get tighter with my cock buried inside of her."

Bernhard thrusts slowly and pushes all of our bodies into the mattress, stopping our momentum momentarily and making Gero hiss in warning again. I've never seen them like this with each other; it sends a thrill through me. They've always had a unique bond that could never be shaken. I admit that my jealousy gets the better of me.

Despite the warning, it doesn't stop Bernhard from shoving his big, hard cock deep inside my ass past the tight muscle. I whimper, mewl, and claw at Gero, trying to adjust to Bernhard's invasion. It feels so full. I'm stretched to the limit, on the precipice of both pain and pleasure, but the only thing my inner voice is chanting is that—it feels *so fucking good. I need more.*

"I can feel your cock right up against mine," Bernhard pants as he places his forehead against my naked back.

"You like feeling me fuck you, Bernhard?"

"Fuck. I do. I love having your cock in my mouth, Gero. You know this."

I lose control of myself, my jealousy spiking again. I sink my teeth into Gero's neck and through his skin. The metallic tang of his blood almost makes my eyes roll back. Gero belongs to me. They both do.

"Idalia," Gero groans.

Bernhard grabs my hair, forces my face off Gero and toward him, slamming his lips on mine. His tongue invades my mouth and tastes the blood that still lingers there. It was probably his plan all along, but my mind soothes the jealous ache by convincing me that he's doing it for me.

"You belong to us, Idalia. I will kill any other man that tries to sniff around you," Bernhard says against my lips. His tongue licks the blood that has trickled down my chin before he pulls back, grabs my hips and digs his fingers into my flesh. "I can't wait any longer."

The men start a different rhythm, quickly setting a brutal pace in both my holes.

"I want your cock in my mouth, Gero. I need to taste you."

"This little omega will be bred," Gero declares, and my pleasure instantaneously increases with his next thrust.

"Would you like that, little omega?" Bernhard whispers. "Do you want me to taste his cum inside of you?"

Gero pulls out and Bernhard pushes in, back and forth they go, overstimulating me into another level of pleasure.

"I'm dying with how you smell right now. You smell so... fucking...good." Bernhard's nose roots against my hair as Gero bites my shoulder over his mark again and tongues the wound, making me moan.

"Please." I don't know what I'm begging for, but I need it soon. I can't take much more of this. My body is about to internally combust being sandwiched between two virile males. Every time Bernhard pushes my body down with his, my clit grinds against Gero beneath me, sparking more and more pleasure. It edges me to the precipice but refuses to take me over, torturing me.

"Idalia, always so greedy," Gero chuckles.

"You like us filling all your holes, don't you?"

My heat is making me want it all. "*Yes!*" I cry out unashamedly.

I need them to fill me up all day, every day. I'm going to make that stupid drink every damn month, until they both realize who they belong to.

"Your pussy is fluttering. *Fuck.* Can you feel how tight she is, Bernhard?"

Bernhard doesn't answer, instead, he growls against my hair and bites down on the other side of my neck, making my pussy clench even more in reaction to his response. Their brutal pace doesn't stop. When Bernhard's teeth pierce my skin, I cry out in pleasure, finally tipping over the edge.

My pussy spasms around them, the muscles of my stomach tightening. It's all too much and not enough at the same time.

They both increase their paces until they start groaning in agony. My body explodes again, and I cry out as both their cocks start to expand in size, spilling inside of me. Two knots are more than I can handle and my initial cries of pleasure border cries of pain, but the haze of my mind and lust make me want more of whatever they have to give me.

"That's it. Such a good little omega," Gero coos. "Fuck, your smell is getting stronger, and it makes me *hungry*."

"We're going to fill you until you're good and bred. Again and again."

"Just the way she likes it, Bernhard. You're such a cum whore, aren't you?" His hand grips my hair and forces my face to tilt up so his tongue can snake into my mouth. Bernhard licks the back of my neck as he continues to thrust into my ass, even though his knot is preventing him from moving much.

Finally, after a wet entanglement of tongues and hands spreading seed all over my pussy lips and thighs, Bernhard falls to the side and pulls me with him, making me yelp from the tugging of Gero's knot inside of me. Turning my face toward him, I bite his collar and suck, extending the pleasure inside of me. *Yes, I guess I am as greedy as they say I am.*

All three of us lay there for who knows how long, my eyes having already drifted closed. I snuggle into Gero's chest and sigh.

"Fuck."

A masculine groan.

"She still smells so good."

The release of the splash between my legs makes me gasp and come awake as the boys rearrange themselves around me, messing up my nest and making me irrationally angry. Growling under my breath, I climb over Gero to fix the pillows as Bernhard chuckles behind me.

Turning around and shooting daggers from my eyes, I bare my teeth. "Laugh it up. You best sleep with one eye open, Bernhard. Stop messing up my nest!"

He growls and pounces on me, making me squeal as his mouth sucks on my breast and his hands pin mine down. He suddenly moves down, pushes my legs up and does as he promised. His tongue dives into my pussy and licks out everything Gero gave me. I should be angry. I should kick him in the face, but I don't. His tongue feels too good. My hand snakes behind his head and pulls his face closer to me, making him take more.

I can hear Gero milling about the room, touching my things. I snap my eyes open, biting my bottom lip to find him cleaning Bernhard with one of their discarded pieces of clothing. Except his hands are moving in a steady pace that's more stroking than anything else as he climbs behind Bernhard and spreads his ass cheeks.

Gero's eyes are on me, dominating, claiming me with just a look. My breath stutters but a new sense of courage courses through me. I grab Bernhard's head, pull him up and slam my lips on his, kissing him passionately.

Gero smirks before he leans over us both and snakes his tongue between us.

It's going to be a long and very fulfilling heat cycle.

8

GERO

We've been locked away in this bedchamber for the past week. Idalia is constantly growling at us and nesting on the bed when we leave to bring food and water. It's cute, but my dick is about to fall off with how much we've been breeding her.

Waking up, I feel someone's mouth on my softened cock, suckling slowly. Without opening my eyes, my hand reaches down to caress the back of Bernhard's head, trying to soothe whatever is agitating him. He's gone through the same changes I have with this heat. What does that say about everything we've come to learn in this world? I now question everything that's been drilled into us, everything about our own biological history. Nothing makes sense yet going through what we went through...everything makes sense. I'm going to have to see what I can find in the castle library.

I lift my eyes to see that Idalia is snoring lightly, buried in sheets and pillows until you can only see her dark hair peek out.

Gently pushing Bernhard away, his arms automatically wrap around me tighter to prevent me from moving. Memories of the dungeon surface and I get a bad taste in my mouth, making the moment turn bittersweet. Finally dislodging him, Bernhard talks in his sleep, turning over to wrap his arm around Idalia's hidden form.

Padding towards the door, I take a few inhales. Idalia is good and bred, judging by the change of scent in the air. Lifting the wooden beam and unlocking the door, I stretch my shoulder muscles after I place the beam onto the ground. It was Bernhard's idea and I'm now glad for it. We never had to use it until her heat. I walk towards the opposite side of the room, where the window sits. Opening the shutters, I look out over my kingdom and smile.

The smile doesn't last when my eyes catch what appears to be a line of dark figures on horses coming our way in the distance, from higher ground. From my memory, the hills are about three to four miles away, our kingdom providing the perfect view of potential threats moving our direction. Grabbing pants and the sword and scabbard off the floor, I belt it around my waist as I slam open Idalia's bedroom door.

Bernhard startles awake, calling my name, but I ignore him as I run down the hall to look for one of the guards or soldiers.

"My Lord!" someone calls out. There's a soldier running down the halls towards this very direction.

"Gero, what's happening?" Bernhard is still naked as he trails behind me.

"Horses. A whole battalion, from what it looks like,

headed our way," I inform him. It's all that I could see, *for now*.

Bernhard curses under his breath as the soldier reaches me and gets down on one knee in respect, but I have no time for etiquette when my gut tells me something bigger than a battalion is coming our way.

"What news do you have for me? Get up!" I command him.

Straightening to his full height, the soldier's face is grim as he delivers the news. "The Northern Kingdom arrives with an army of thousands."

"Shit. Gero, what do we do?"

Without looking at Bernhard, I answer him. "The only thing we can do. Call all the men to gather their arms, both alphas and betas."

It's not a surprise this day would come. It is why I've been gathering more troops and pushing for more training.

"Yes, my Lord."

I watch as the soldier turns and runs. My mind spins with battle strategies I've heard about through talks between the men of the previous regime while I was still but a servant to the Alpha's omega. Growing up in a poor village, my grandfather's time was the last time there was military conscription. It seems history is going to have to repeat itself in order for us to gather enough men to refill our army.

"Gero, what are you thinking? What's the plan? What do you need me to do?"

I turn to Bernhard with a determination I haven't felt since our uprising. "My friend, the only thing we can do. Prepare for war."

I lead Bernhard towards the battle room, but not before

pointing to his naked cock swinging between his legs to let him know he needs to gear up.

Catching the eye of a random guard standing against the wall, I point my finger. "You! Gather the commanders and tell them to meet me in the battle room for an emergency strategy meeting."

"Yes, my Lord."

"Bernhard, find a messenger. Send a missive to all the villages in the kingdom. The time has come for mandatory military conscription. We need to increase our numbers quickly."

"The Northern Kingdom will be here before we can train the villagers," Bernhard replies while strapping himself up with weapons and calling for the stable boy.

"We're going to have to take that risk. Our current military will have to hold them off for as long as they can before they can reach the outlying villages."

A feminine voice cuts through our conversation. "Gero! Bernhard?"

My head snaps towards the sound of Idalia's voice, and then to her stomach with possessiveness. "Idalia, find the other omegas and hole yourselves in the heart of the palace. Wait for me to come for you."

"W-what's going on?" The worry in her eyes makes my chest feel something I'm unable to name.

"War is coming from the north. You just worry about your safety, let us handle the rest."

She stares at me, but this time not in defiance, with another emotion. "Okay."

She runs off, and my cock chooses that exact moment to

twitch as I watch her ass move in her dress. *I bet my cock still smells like her slick.*

Bernhard slaps my back, stealing my attention before grinning. Shaking my head, we continue our path toward the battle room to find five alphas waiting for us with scowls. The only reason they're here and not in the dungeons is because they agreed to pledge loyalty to me.

"We haven't had war on our doorsteps in years, yet here we are," His eyes speak volumes, without being uttered out loud. He blames my reign for this war.

Little does he know, I am not one to back down. Not now. Not when there are more important matters than snide remarks from grown men. "It doesn't matter who's on the throne, war comes when it comes and waits for no man. It's up to us as a whole to prepare for what's to come, and to defend our kingdom. Wouldn't you agree, Commander Drust?"

It's been easy to control the soldiers under their command once the betas and omegas decided to side with me in this new reign. The commanders, however, are a different story. They choose to remain civil, but their demeanor speaks the truth every time we cross paths.

My patience is thin due to my recent rut with Idalia, my body feeling changes after a week of being locked away. The scent of my simmering anger starts to permeate the air, making the other alphas in the room grumble under their breath instead of being direct.

"We've already discussed battle strategies. We need to take them by surprise from the behind, while using a decoy group in the front. Archers will be hidden on the sides to slow down the militia if they come upon our decoy too quickly. The decoy will all be ground soldiers who specialize in hand to hand." Commander Egil leans on the table, where a map of the kingdom has already been spread out.

I stare at the two major kingdoms to the east and the Northern Kingdom which rivals the size of ours.

I've studied the map a time or two, but not enough to understand the layout for the best possible scenario of winning a war. Celebrations of freedom with Bernhard have distracted me. I'm going to have to fix that.

The others in the room murmur their agreement with Commander Egil and proceed to speak about which team will be sent where. Coordination of the soldiers comes easy, each commander understanding his place in the game and what their battalion brings to the table in this upcoming war. None of them mention the newly acquired soldiers from the villages.

It's not a fact I bring up, not when they're all deep in tactics. I say the only thing I can in the moment. "Inform me the moment the men are scheduled to deploy."

"Yes, my Lord," one of the commanders sneer under his breath. My eyes cut to him and my nostrils flare. That's a problem for another day. He will be made an example after this war is over.

Priorities.

Exiting the battle room without another word, my feet lead me, without a thought of my own, down the hallway towards the heart of the palace. Thoughts of Idalia run through my mind, the many ways she could be in danger being connected with me. Now that she possibly carries my child—our child—she must be protected at all costs.

Bernhard hasn't followed me. I assume he has gone to

ready the horses and speak with the betas about what has been discussed in the battle room. My footsteps are the only sound to be heard as I take a left along the next hallway.

Suddenly, the hairs on the back of my neck stand and I pull out my sword and swing in the direction my instincts are pointing me.

An enemy infiltration and no one knows about it? How can this be?

The vibration of the parry travels down my arms and into my very bones upon impact as my sword clashes with the newcomer who's covered from head to toe in black, blending him into the shadows.

"You dare enter the halls of my kingdom?" I snarl in his face.

He narrows his eyes and jumps back. In quick succession, our swords dance and clash once more, sending sparks toward the ground. The sound of metal-on-metal echoes down the halls.

"There is no alpha ruling here." The voice is distorted and low, as if it's being processed through magic, or something else.

Growling, I use my full body weight on the next swing, dominating the parry, bending his body backward as I bare my teeth and snap it in front of his face. The expression in his eyes does not falter. The rest of his face is covered in black cloth, hiding the rest of his features.

Quickly, he jerks to the side, dislodging my sword and jumps a foot back. The male is light on his feet, giving him the agility to duck and roll, evading my next upward swing. Another body comes crashing into the newcomer like a cannon, the sound of his snarl and roar a familiar one.

Bernhard's hand-to-hand combat with his ax knocks the sword out of the enemy's grasp, providing him with a window of opportunity to head butt and stun him. The stranger falls onto his back with a loud thud and doesn't move. Bernhard shifts his gaze to me, waiting for my command with impatience. I don't give him one. Instead, I walk over and bend down to pull off the mask, trying to identify where he hails from. Without warning, Bernhard surprisingly growls again and quickly sinks his teeth into the other male's face, ripping the flesh off without warning.

Well, there goes that.

I don't blame him. A threat this close to the omegas—this close to ours—makes my blood boil with the need for retribution. When I lean over to grab the hilt of the fallen sword, I see rubies and topazes encrusted on the handle. Growing up in a poor village, we're not as literate in house crests and colors as those of the aristocracy of the kingdom. Memorizing the gems, I hear my name being called and turn my head.

Idalia runs towards me and only gives me a moment to drop the enemy's sword as she jumps into my arms in a tight embrace. She buries her face into my neck, inhaling deeply, her entire body trembling. My chest momentarily constricts with discomfort.

"I-I thought I was going to lose you! You asshole! Don't ever do that to me! *I need you!*"

Chuckling at her antics, I nuzzle the top of her head as Bernhard stands up from his crouch over the dead body with blood dripping down his lips and chin. His smile is feral as he walks towards us and pulls Idalia into his arms, kissing her deeply.

This is only the beginning. If one was able to breach, who's to say more will not? My body tenses up with agitation at something I'm not seeing. My senses are still heightened from the surprise attack.

"Bernhard, return Idalia to the safety of the room. I need to have word with one of the commanders about what happened here."

He licks her bloodied face and doesn't spare me a look. "Yes, my Lord."

Watching them walk away, my mind plays over the last thing the male said. How did news of Edelgard's fall move so swiftly across the lands to the other surrounding territories, when the news is still barely reaching the villages on the outskirts of this kingdom?

And how did they know to target me and not some other beta when the castle is now full of ex prisoners?

There's only one way news would fly that fast.

We have a traitor in our midst.

Swiftly heading out the castle walls, I make my way toward the servants' quarters that are housing the new recruits. Soldiers and guards are bustling through the courtyard as they all complete the commands they were given. I make it through the servants' doors, looking around the sea of faces, to find a familiar one.

"Cyprian. Ivo."

Two dark heads snap toward my direction.

"Split the recruits into two teams. They will be manning the castle as the others are sent out further. Where's Philon?"

Cyprian looks around the room before swinging his gaze back to me. "He was here a moment ago. Perhaps he's gone to look for Raban."

Of course. In times of discourse, we cling onto what subconsciously reminds us of comfort and safety.

"See to it that each man here knows their duty to the kingdom. We don't know if the Northern Kingdom will make it this far, but we must prepare for it regardless. We must protect the heart of the castle at all costs."

"Yes, my Lord."

Ivo nods in agreement right before he belts out commands over the new recruits who are nervously moving around. Ducking my head out of the servants' quarters, I make my way toward the armory. The sound of hammer on metal and the heat of the room slams into me right before I enter.

"Raban!"

The hammering continues.

"Raban!"

The beta growls and jerks off his helm. "What?"

I scrutinize his face and the way his muscles bulge under his shirt. Has he also started to change?

"We need more weapons within the next few days. An army approaches."

He shucks his project into the forge and throws his gloved hands into the air, cursing over the open flame. Grabbing his large metal tongs with a bright red tip, he points it at me. "*My Lord*, I will have your bloody weapons! Now leave my forge!"

A laugh erupts from my gut, and I throw my head back. The servant boy who's been quietly sitting in the corner startles and falls off his stool, clattering the weapons near him onto the floor.

"Bloody hell!" Raban tosses his tongs down and stalks over to the chaos behind him.

Shaking my head, I leave and make my way to the stables to see if I can catch Bernhard before he leaves. Walking past soldiers gearing up in Edelgard's colors makes my skin prickle, but we have no choice. We didn't have time to tailor the new uniforms. This also leaves the question of the kingdom's treasury, something I have yet to venture into and question. Will we have enough to fund this war if it comes to that? I guess we'll find out soon enough.

The stables are half empty when I arrive. My temper spikes at the fact that I missed his departure. Slamming my fist against one of the stable walls, I trudge back to the heart of the castle. Idalia is going to have to calm me down before I am able to address the alphas again.

9

IDALIA

It's been about a week since Bernhard left. I've never seen Gero this feral. The way he plows into me as if he wants to kill me and tear my soul apart. The way his mouth devours mine in dominance as his muscles flex around me, drilling his hard cock inside of my womb.

We're both sweating, gliding against each other's naked bodies when a rumble comes from deep within his chest, vibrating all the way down to my pussy, pushing me over the edge I've been riding for the past thirty minutes. I cry out but Gero swallows it down, diving his tongue into my mouth, forcing me to give him everything. I bite him and he purrs harder, slapping his hips against me until finally locking and spilling himself inside.

How did we ever mistake him for a beta? In fact, how can something like this happen at all? It's not natural, is it? Everything I ever thought I knew is now challenged by this man before me. He's not the man who served under me.

Whatever happened in the dungeons has transformed him into something *more*.

We continue to kiss passionately with the taste of his blood between us. His large hands firmly grip onto my naked ass, forcing me to grind against him. When a finger swirls in our combined wetness and slips into my back entrance, I mewl and relax into his ministrations.

I yelp and jump when a knock comes at the door behind us. Gero slaps his hand over my mouth and continues to grind against me, growling.

The knock comes again and Gero snaps, "What?"

The voice on the other side of the door isn't perturbed. "My Lord, you're needed."

His cock is still spilling inside of me. We are against the shelves that hold the fuel for torches in this small storage closet. Gero grabbed me and threw me in here the moment we crossed paths without a single word exchanged. I didn't question him and I'm glad for it. I want him to always seek me and my body for comfort and release.

"My Lord. A missive has been sent addressed to you from Bernhard."

Suddenly, Gero's knot releases and he slips out. Quickly tucking himself away and fastening his pants, he jerks the wooden door open and leaves.

"When did it arrive?" he asks from farther away.

The sound of muffled voices is all I hear as I try to rearrange myself before exiting. Smoothing down my hair, I take a deep inhale when I step back into the castle halls.

Flustered, I quickly make my way through the opposite side away from their exit and toward my bedroom.

"Idalia? Are you okay? You look a little..." one of the

chambermaids asks curiously, but her eyes tell me she knows exactly what happened.

I've seen her a few times. Emma. Fair skin and innocent green eyes. She usually works with the servants who handle the laundry. I'm sure she's been one of the ones handling ours during my heat.

I give her a quick smile and quickly walk past her. When I make it to my bedroom, I shut the door and freshen myself by splashing water on my face and neck. Gently wiping the droplets away with a terry cloth, a knock comes at my door.

"Madam, a missive has arrived addressed to you."

What in the world? No one has ever written to me, not since I was taken from my village as one of Edelgard's omegas. Curious, I turn around and open the door for the servant. He has his head bent in a semi bow with his hand out and holding a little piece of paper. I've never seen him before. Perhaps he came in with the group that Bernhard brought back.

I take it from him, thank him, and shut the door.

Scrunching my brows in confusion, I slowly unfold the sheet and recognize my mother's writing.

Idalia,

I hope this letter finds you quickly and that life as an omega within the castle walls has been good to you. I've been able to settle your father's debts with the generous amount Lord Edelgard has sent each month.

But I haven't received a payment this prior cycle and the animals need their feed. Your father attempted to barter off the pig while gambling and I fear that I may have to remove myself from him before he can bury us in his problems once more.

News has flown through Seaton that a new leader has risen to power. While I am unsure if the rumors are true, the lack of funding for this prior month has led me to believe so for it is the only explanation. Since you have not returned home and since there has not been any rumors of your departure, I assume you still live within the castle walls.

Find it in your heart to help the woman who bore you into this world.

-Mum

She cannot be serious. How did I not know that Edelgard essentially sent her a bride price for me? Nothing was ever mentioned during my time here but after reading her letter, I can logically see why. He didn't want her coming back for me after essentially stealing me away.

What does she mean my father attempted to barter off the pig? She's never had animals and my father has never been a gambler. My mother sold herbs and tinctures just as my grandmother did. It's how this whole situation came to be.

"How peculiar..." I mumble to myself.

I'm left with more questions than answers as I refold the note and walk over to my table to place it under my box of jewels.

My paranoia increases, but I say nothing as I walk over to my window and look out over the soldiers that spar and practice battle formations in the grassy courtyard. My eyes track to the dark mountains and stare at what looks like tents that have been erected a few miles out.

"Tighten formation men! Precision intimidates the enemy. We need to present ourselves as a solid front!"

The sound of boots and shields continue to float from below.

I do not understand the business of men, but the Northern army's decision to bunker down so close to our kingdom seems to be an aggressive and forward move on their part. I stare at the flickers of blues and purples flapping in the wind. Wasn't Edelgard meeting with the North? Had something gone awry before the meeting and his demise?

History has spoken about our past enemies with tales of victory on our part after they threatened to take our lands as their own under their makeshift belief that they had been ordained by a higher power as the chosen people to rule all nations. That was only a few decades past. They've successfully swallowed half of the Draxt Nation to the west after sending missionaries in that direction to convince the locals of their religious proselytizing.

Many initially believed in their evangelizing until they took darker measures to convert the people who were not conforming to their ways. It was easy for them to conquer the villages and towns they were always stationed in through a sudden inquisition.

Was this the method they were trying with us?

"That wouldn't make any sort of sense whatsoever," I tell myself aloud.

The moment the thought left my lips is the moment my door opens. "Who are you speaking to, Idalia?"

I turn around and lean my hands behind me against the window. "Gero. Is everything alright? What did Bernhard say?"

He stares at me for a moment with a blank expression. I can never tell where I stand with Gero. I know he enjoys my body, but most days he seems to hate the fact that he does. I shouldn't be jealous of his relationship with Bernhard, but when his eyes bore into mine as if he's trying to peek at my soul, I can't help myself.

What does he see?

Does he see a woman who has fallen at his feet trying to survive this life? Or does he see an annoyance and a pastime?

"Northern missionaries have been seen through the town of Borough, three hundred miles from here."

My eyes widen. "Have they come to take our lands? Will this be another Draxt Nation problem?" What does this mean for the Southern Kingdom? What will this mean for us?

Gero steps toward me until we're toe to toe, towering over my form. His presence is overpowering as well as his scrutiny.

"Who sent you a message from Borough?"

I gulp. Why does he sound like I'm about to be destroyed? "M-My mother."

Gero leans in further and places his hands on either side of mine behind me on the windowsill, caging me in.

"Why now, Omega? Why does your mother send you a message now?"

I silently shake my head. "I honestly don't know. And it doesn't sound like my mother."

His eyes narrow as he scans my face from my eyes to my lips. My heart is racing. Is he going to throw me out the window, glass be damned? My face flames when he closes the distance but glides to the side, his cheek against mine, the scruff of his face scraping my skin deliciously.

"Make no mistake, Omega. You belong to me. But I will not hesitate to punish you if I must."

His voice is throaty, gruff, and I can't help the slick that runs down my legs. I can hear and feel him inhaling my hair and it makes goosebumps rise and my breath stutter.

"Give me the letter, Idalia."

Lost in his command, I quickly scramble to grab the paper from under my box of jewels and hand it to him with doe eyes.

He grins as he gently takes it from me, scrambling my mind in confusion. His smile falls as he stares at the letter and my heart rate kicks up even more. What's going on in his mind?

Folding it back, he turns and walks out of my room without another word.

I'm scared. For all my bluster and aspirations, Gero is unpredictable. The simple fact that in the blink of an eye, he was able to lead a group of prisoners and take down our Alpha keeps me in fear.

My hopes of having him between my legs to control that unpredictability is vanishing into thin air the longer I stare at my bedroom door.

I can't stay here.

Quickly turning, I frantically rummage through my things and pack up a bag for my exit from the castle tonight. I can't trust anyone. Gero will make good on his threat, and by the time Bernhard returns, it might be too late for me. It doesn't matter if any fault lies with me or not. It is the way of the world. Men have the power to hold a woman's life in their hands.

With tears streaming down my cheeks, I scratch and claw at the stone wall beneath my window, trying to dislodge the loose rock. My hands are shaking, and it doesn't help matters.

The sound of weapons and sparring float through my window as I wipe my face with my shoulder and try again. With a small growl, I dig my fingers down, sending pain through my nail beds, and pull hard. I fall backwards with a yelp, but the rock is completely removed.

Crawling on hands and knees, I stick my right arm in and feel around. Skipping irrelevant items like my mortar and pestle, I reach to the far right until I can feel a velvet satchel. I have to push my forearm against the small hole in order to be able to reach the tie string on tip with my index and middle fingers.

I quickly pull it out and hiss when my skin scrapes against the jagged edge of the opening. Small pink streaks mar my skin but I ignore the throbbing as I open the bag and pour it into my left palm.

Out falls a few jewels, gold, and coins. The golden chain can be broken into pieces if it must in order for me to use it as a form of trade.

"The army is camped to the north. I can't go back home to Borough, Gero will follow me there because of the letter," I mumble to myself, trying to figure out my best route with what I have to travel. My tanned skin would never pass for a Northerner, not where their manes are reminiscent of the color of wheat.

There's no way around it. I will run out of payment before I can make it far enough. I need to secure a horse.

Drawing the bag closed, I jump up and make my way to my wardrobe. Opening the doors, I look around to see what I can pack and wear for my quick escape. Among the frills and finery, hidden behind a stack of stockings and underthings, I've kept my old clothes from home.

The young girl from the past didn't know this day would come, but she was paranoid enough to make an exit plan regardless.

"Miss Idalia, you look quite stunning tonight. Has the Lord spoken with you about what's to come for our kingdom? What are our plans for the army to the north?"

I tip my chalice back with a shy smile, taking a sip of the wine. "Ladies aren't privy to such matters. Especially omegas. I am unsure myself, but I do know that my Lord will find a way to handle the situation. After all, our own military has increased in preparation for such a day."

One of the betas that has been promoted to oversee the housing for the new recruits looks at me with curiosity. I don't like it. I don't like the way he makes me feel when he speaks to me.

"You are quite an obedient omega. Anyone would be honored to have such a beauty by his side."

Suddenly, the hairs on the back of my neck stand on end and I take another swallow of wine, staring at the inside of my chalice. He reminds me of a serpent, waiting for the right time to strike with his truth. I'm not stupid enough to let myself fall victim to whatever game he is playing in front of everyone to see.

Gero's anger can be felt in the air and the beta's eyes sharpen before turning back to his dinner plate.

"Idalia, finish your meal and head back to your quarters.

I will meet you there after my meeting with the commanders."

The perfect save. "Yes, my Lord."

I grab the napkin from my lap, dab my mouth, push back on my chair, and remove myself from the room with my eyes cast down. The air is so thick it could be cut with a butter knife, and I gladly make my way out the throne room and into the adjoining hall. The tapestry lined halls have a few guards that stand at attention with armor, but they pay me no mind. I slow my steps and walk with my head held high until I reach my bedchambers.

Shutting the door, I lean back against it and let out a relieved breath. Quickly gathering myself, I get to work on removing my outer clothing. I decide to keep my inside slip and a layer of skirt for warmth before redressing with my dull brown clothes. Loosing my hair from its confines, I rebraid it tightly and pin it up against my head.

Dropping to my knees, I reach under my bed for the prepared pack. I was able to grab some extra biscuits and dried meats from the omegas in the kitchen with the excuse of pregnancy cravings.

The carpet rug beneath my bed makes it difficult to drag the pack out, but I am able to with a few jerks. Throwing it onto my back, I grab one of my scarves and tuck it into my pocket. I'll use it once I leave the castle grounds in order to help hide my face until I make it to the next town.

Straightening, I walk to my window and look out at the moonlit sky. It's the perfect night. There's enough light to help me find my way. The shadows of the trees that surround us will help hide me enough to slip through.

I haven't been outside of the castle walls since my arrival, but I recall there is an outer stone perimeter and metal gate leading to the front. I'll just have to figure out that obstacle when I get there.

Quietly slipping through my door, I tiptoe out the hallway and into one of the linen closets. I wait for the sound of footsteps from the patrolling guards to go by before I slip out the door and head toward one of the hidden entrances inside the walls.

Memories of Edelgard's untimely demise hit me like a ton of bricks, but I keep moving forward. *I loved him as an omega should, but I didn't truly love him at all, did I?* The air is cool within the walls, the smell of wet stone surrounds me. Was it only a few months past since the takeover—since Gero took over my life?

The phantom sensation of him claiming me a few hours ago makes my pussy throb. Shaking my head, I try to concentrate on my task. The intricate tunnels of the inside walls have me lost for a few moments, but I'm able to redirect myself towards the outside. The secret exit door takes me to one of the servant's quarters. Luckily, it's empty. The new recruits have already been put into position to patrol the perimeter.

Quietly making my way to the front door, I look left and right. No one is about. Slipping out, I fast walk toward the stables.

Memories of my meeting a few days ago run through my mind.

"Hello."

The young stable boy jumps when he hears my voice, turning quickly with his hand over his heart. He chuckles when he notices it's only me, another omega.

"Miss Idalia! What are you doing out in the stables? This is no place for a lady such as yourself."

I bat my eyelashes and coo, "I was just curious and bored. I wanted to see the majestic creatures the soldiers ride on. I haven't ridden one myself, but always wanted to."

I lied. During my childhood in Borough, my family and I rode on horseback to many different towns in order to seek trade and make a living. My mother and grandmother with their tinctures, my father with his skill as a huntsman, selling pelt.

The stable boy looks surprised and honored that I have come to him with my curiosity. I let him speak excitedly of saddles and the taming of horses while I scope out the one that would suit my plan best.

There, in the second to last stable, is a smaller brown horse that would suit my size best.

Finally excusing myself from the stables, I curtsey and politely ask if I can come by another time.

"Yes, yes, of course my Lady! I'd love to have your company. Whatever questions you have, feel free to ask me and I will be more than happy to answer you the best I can. I come from a long line of stable masters, my father being one of the best I know who used to serve the prior King."

"You are too kind. But I may take you up on your offer. We'll just keep this a secret between us, okay?"

His eyes widen comically, only now realizing the predicament he has found himself in. Gero's possessiveness over me has been slowly making itself known throughout the staff.

"Yes, yes. Of course, my lady. As you wish. Please, I don't want to lose my position here. I know nothing but the stables. I've come to love these horses as if they were my own."

Patting him on the shoulder, he flinches but hangs his head in defeat. "I understand, Sebastian. You need not worry for long."

Walking past him, I don't look back and don't elaborate on my final words.

"There you are," I coo at the mare. She whinnies, but I shush her and place my hand over her nose, gently stroking. "It's okay. We're going to take a little trip, you and I. Would you like that? Just us girls."

Her eyes are intelligent though and she makes not a sound as I grab one of the nearby saddles and place it over her back. Grabbing one of the fruits from my bag, I lure her out of her stall and give her a treat.

While she eats, I settle myself on top of her and grip the reins. Steering her out, she obediently follows my command, and we slip into the shadows.

IO

IDALIA

The outer gate is taller than I remember. Pulling the reins to the left, I move my mare along the wall to see if there are any other exit points.

"Do you think the Northern Kingdom will send in secret assassins while they distract us with their encampments?"

"Didn't you hear? Someone already breached the castle."

"What? What happened to them?" the first soldier stops to ask. Both soldiers are standing in my way a few feet ahead. Hiding behind one of the trees and bushes, I gently pat my mare to keep her quiet and calm.

"It seems someone ripped his face off."

Soldier number one gulps and croaks out, "W-was our new Lord, Gero?"

"I don't know the details. All I know is that the infiltrator was quickly dealt with and that's when we all heard the news of the Northern march."

"Are we sure our new king is in his right mind? They say

he was a prisoner, locked away for misdeeds and kept like an animal in the dark."

The second soldier chastised the first. "Don't speak of such things out loud, Koen."

"Why not? It's just us out here. Don't tell me you haven't thought the same."

"It doesn't matter what I think. We are to secure the perimeter for tonight until the changing of the guard. Keep your mind on your duty, would you?"

"I am, I am."

The sound of their boots on the grass softly *thuds* further away. My hand continues to stroke the mare's mane until I can no longer hear them. Gently nudging her with my heel, I pull the reins and move her in the direction where the guards were just standing.

The wall in front of us towers about five feet above my head, completely made of stone. How in the world will I make it over with a horse in tow? There must be a back gate somewhere. It would be stupid to only have a front entrance.

Slowly trotting along the shadows of the wall, I hear a whisper and snap my head to the side in a panic.

"Psst," comes again.

To my surprise, it's Sebastian. What is he doing here?

I wave my hand at him to shoo him away. He doesn't leave. Instead, he comes out from the shadows of the bush he's behind and runs up to me, making my heart beat out of my chest in fear. What if we're caught?

"My Lady. I promise you; no one knows but me and I will take your secret to the grave. Please, take this letter to Harden village. Hand it to my brother, Giles. Giles Walter. I beg of you."

I don't have time for this!

As if he can read my thoughts, his next words make me stop. "I know of an exit. They bring in the new horses through there. Please, just take my letter and I will show you the way."

"Why are you helping me?"

Sebastian is already grabbing the reins and pulling my horse along a path I don't recognize. "I know not what kind of life you've led inside these walls, my lady. But any woman who has *this* much courage in escaping a man that killed our previous alpha must be desperate for good reason."

I say nothing. Instead, I'm sifting through my mind to see if I even know where the village of Harden is. After weaving through the small labyrinth behind the courtyard, the sounds of crickets and the horse's soft footfalls are the only thing that accompany us as we make our way toward a secret gate just beyond the maze.

"Trade goods for the kitchen also come through here, so be careful, my Lady. Though nothing runs at this odd hour of the night, you still need to watch yourself. If anyone asks, I will say that the mare lost her way after someone left her stall unlatched."

"Thank you. Truly." And I mean it. This night would have been a failure if it wasn't for Sebastian. What would Gero have done if he knew I was trying to leave in the middle of the night? He's probably searching the castle for me even now.

As if on cue, a murderous, masculine roar rings out into the night sky, silencing the insects and nighttime creatures, and sending a chill up my spine. The horse whinnies, but Sebastian is able to calm her before she gets too loud.

"You must hurry! Harden is a village directly south of here, right off the Clement inlet. Please!"

All I can do is nod as I swiftly pull the reins to the right as Sebastian runs to open the iron gate just big enough for me and the horse.

Ride swift is the last thing I hear as I exited the castle walls, and escape into the great unknown.

I didn't have a destination in mind, but south it is. It is better to be farther away from whatever is happening in the North right now.

GERO

"Where is she?" I roar at the guards in her hallway. My fist lands on the wall next to his head, and he shrinks in his armor only further pissing me off. How did she slip away so easily? First the assassin and now this!

"How can a simple omega slip through your fingers? What is the point of putting you all on guard?"

The men visibly gulp, and it aggravates me even more. I feel as if I'm losing control. I can't. Not when the kingdom needs it the most. Not when I need her to keep me together when I mentally want to fall apart.

A statement needs to be made and it needs to be done now.

Grabbing the tunic of the closest beta, I grit out an order.

"Bring me every single person Idalia spoke to today and take them to the dungeons. *Now.*"

He pales but frantically nods his head. "Y-Yes, my Lord."

"NOW!" I bark as I shove him against the guard and they both topple to the ground in a pathetic heap.

I'm losing it. Without Bernhard here and now without Idalia, my patience is nonexistent. Stomping back into Idalia's chambers, I take in sharp inhales as I rummage through her things, scattering it about. Memories of her spit-fire anger at disrupting her nest make my chest ache with longing. Her scent is still strong. With every toss of the sheet, the smell of her hits me in waves. She hasn't been gone that long. Where could she have gone? Why did she feel the need to flee? Does she not realize the predicament she is in as a pregnant omega?

I growl as I tear into one of her stupid frilly pillows.

I couldn't read the letter from her mother. I didn't yet want to expose the fact that I'm illiterate and that I needed to seek out Ivo for assistance.

Once I found out the contents of the letter, it only increased my paranoia about something coming our way. Earlier today, I eavesdropped on a few of the commanders congregating in a separate room just off from the south side of the castle and found out that Edelgard had a previously planned meeting with the North before his death. Could this be it? The reason why they've come this far down? But why bring an entire army for just a simple meeting?

No. This is something else.

Where the hell is Idalia when I need her? I fist her scattered dress from the bed and lift it to my nose, inhaling deeply. She still smells like us, and it calms me for a few seconds.

"Where are you, little Omega?"

She could be out there starving our child, and that alone puts me in a new kind of blind rage. Angrily throwing her dress on the bed, I slam her door against the wall and single mindedly head to the one place I never wanted to see or smell again.

I can vaguely hear my name being called, but I can't respond. My jaw is locked from me gritting my teeth as I continue to descend downward the stairwell until the walls smell of mold and wet stone.

The air of death and hopelessness threatens to seep into my bones with each step. The torches flicker with the speed of my descent and I stop just long enough to grab one on my way down. The shadows dance with the flame and it takes me a moment to fully accept the fact that I'm now on the other side, no longer behind the prison bars.

The sound of chains rattling drifts to my ears and my head twitches. It grates on my nerves as well as comforts me with its familiarity. When I make it to the bottom, two of the prison guards greet me with respectful nods and I ignore them, heading straight to my destination.

Some of the alphas are already standing at the bars, staring at me with crossed arms and aggressive stances as I pace back and forth looking for my next victim. It's their fault we're in this predicament.

"What kind of meeting was made with the North? Why now?"

"Why should we tell you anything? You are nothing but scum that wants to play king," one of them snarls.

I slam my palm on the bars, baring my teeth. "Guards!"

Alvo and Thovy quickly run to my side and unlock the door. They were part of the betas that served in the main part of the castle as servants. I stationed them here while the rest of us acclimated back into civilization.

Swinging it open, I grab the scruff of the prisoner's shirt and pull him out, tossing him to the ground.

"Lock the doors."

"Yes, my Lord," Thovy quickly replied.

Alvo stands by and watches my every move with a blank expression.

The prisoner, someone I do not remember in the rage fueled state I'm in, tries to grab my ankle but I leap enough for his hand to miss and for me to kick him in the head, stunning him.

"You're the king of nothing! We will rise again, just you wait, Beta," one of the other ones growls behind me.

I look over my shoulder, my vision clouded with nothing but the need to punish. "Wait your turn, *Alpha*. It'll come soon enough."

Leaning down, I grab him from the back of his shirt and drag him towards the one room we all tried our best to avoid.

"You're making a big mistake. You'll regret the day you escaped."

"Oh, I regret alright. I regret the moment I didn't kill you all."

"Shut it, ya skamelar!"

"What did you just call me?"

I ignore the grunts and arguments that follow, knowing full well that Alvo is controlling the situation I left behind.

Thovy's footsteps can be heard following me as I continue to drag the body of whoever this is on the ground.

We make it through the short dark tunnel. Thovy was smart enough to bring a torch with us, lighting the way into the next room. The moment we reach it is the moment the smell hits my nose. It reeks of piss and fear. Old, rusted cuffs hang from the walls and a thick wooden table sits in the middle.

Thovy places the torch on the wall and comes over to me, waiting for my command.

"Grab his legs."

"Yes, my Lord."

We both heft him over onto the table and strap him down with the thick leather belts attached to the sides. Edelgard sometimes took a few of us back here, only to return by himself. In silence, we knew exactly what went on beyond the tunnel.

"What's his name?" I ask Thovy, still unable to pull him from my memory.

"Palasar. He was the royal treasurer."

My face splits into a grin. The treasurer bluffs like the rest of the alphas. This is exactly why things need to change. All talk and the outer villages still remain poor while those behind the castle walls live in luxury.

I turn to look about the room. A raggedy table catches my eye and I make my way toward it to find rusted tools for torture. Yes, this will do.

The smell of piss fades away as my senses adapt to it. Grabbing what looks like a serrated awl, I make my way back to Palasar's side. He moans as he rolls his head side to side, coming back into awareness.

I shove the pointed end of the awl straight into his collarbone, making him cry out in agony.

"Awake now, Princess? It's rude to keep guests waiting."

"You parasite! I'll kill you!"

I chuckle at his threat. "Is that what you're doing? Tell me why Edelgard planned to meet with the North."

He spits in my face, and I jerk my head back, wiping it away with the back of my hand.

"I'll tell you nothing. Let the kingdom fall under your rule and the people will see why alphas need to lead."

I shove the awl deeper, the serrated edge pulling at his flesh and creating a dirty wound. When he opens his mouth to scream, I shove my fist inside, locking his jaw open.

He bites down and I grit my teeth. Despite his attempt, his jaw is hinged too wide to do any severe damage. I lean in and give him a feral smile.

"You've caught me at a bad time you see. I'm a little frustrated and my little omega is nowhere to be found to ease my ache. Seems, you'll have to do."

His eyes widen as he tries to flail his arms and legs with no success.

"Thovy, get me a sword."

"Y-Yes, my Lord." He quickly leaves the room and my smile falls. My anger permeates the air, making it thick and oppressing. It's something new that I can't wrap my head around just yet. All these changes are happening too quickly —from within and without. My muscles bunch in tension as I continuously shove the awl in and out like a cock through the flesh around his collarbone.

He moans disgustingly and I take my fist out of his mouth, wiping his spittle onto his dirty tunic.

"You crazy, Be—"

He gurgles. His blood fills his mouth, spilling out the sides and pooling under him as I shove the awl deeper into the side of his neck. Despite two bodies occupying this room, it remains cold, the complete opposite to the tumultuous inferno that rolls inside of me.

"You better control that anger, boy. Know your place beneath me."

My father's voice floats through my mind. Remnants of a previous life. My place is no longer beneath anyone, especially not this pathetic excuse of an alpha.

"I tire of pointless conversations. My father always told me that actions speak louder than words, wouldn't you agree?"

He doesn't answer me. Not the way Idalia always does with her annoying comebacks. Not the way Idalia does when she tries to pacify my anger and succeeds without realizing it.

How could she leave me? How could she leave us?

"My Lord?" Thovy shakily asks. When did he get back?

I stick out my hand and wait. He places the sword's hilt in my palm, and I roll my neck, weighing the balance of the weapon in my grip with the sound of our former treasurer drowning in his own blood.

"You may go, Thovy," I say with subdued menace. A strange calm washes over me.

"Yes, my Lord."

I don't watch to see if he leaves. Instead, I grab the sword with both hands and lift it over my head.

"Where the hell is she?" I bark at myself and no one as I bring down the blade and slice through his thigh, stopping halfway through the bone. The blood splashes and spurts out like a fountain of life.

Idalia carries life within her.

Growling, I jerk the blade back and bring it down once more with all the fury I can muster. The blade cracks the bone and lodges into the wooden table underneath and I roar out with frustration.

When I find that little omega, she's going to pay. She's going to pay dearly.

II

IDALIA

A few hours in and I slow the horse to a trot, patting the side of her neck and looking for a location to camp for the night. The light of the moon is barely visible, only enough for me to see a few feet ahead. The next town south is Thatchum, according to the map I was able to glance at.

This is going to be dangerous. I haven't ventured to the outlying villages before. Will they question me? An omega who's pregnant and heavy with the scent of...

"Stupid, Idalia. You need to get as far away as possible, not think of them," I mumble to myself in reassurance. I need to see this plan through. I can't go back. Not when my mother's letter might put me at risk. Would Bernhard see me as a threat? Gero is known to be paranoid, but perhaps it's my own wariness that sees him that way.

No matter. The decision has been made and I'm already here.

137

We walk along beside the thick trees, weaving in and out for coverage. The crunch of leaves is soft under the horse's footfalls and, thankfully, damp from the fog that surrounds us.

"You'll be able to warn me of any predators, won't you? We might as well find a good patch of leaves to rest for the night."

The horse whinnies and continues forward.

"How about that spot right there?" I point to what looks like a small opening to a cave.

Directing the horse that way, I slide off her back and onto my feet. Gripping the reins in my hand, I lead her further in. The mouth of the cave is dark. Fear of the unknown grips me, but fear of death by Gero's hands pushes me forward.

Bending down at the mouth of the cave, I grip a sizable stone and toss it in. The sound of the rock bouncing echoes for a short time.

"Not that deep then. We might be okay. What do you think, girl?"

Of course, the horse doesn't answer.

With what I could see, I gather as many branches and twigs as I could, piling them right at the mouth of the cave. Dried leaves are placed on top to help with kindling. Pulling one of the matches I packed, I swipe it against stone and toss it into the pile.

Smoke grows into embers as I blow against the flames with cupped hands. Soon enough a small, warm flame grows, and I lean back against the wall of the cave.

Snacking on some of what I packed, I don't see the threat until it is already here.

"Well, well, well. Aldo, can you believe our luck?"

"An omega, out here? What are you doing all on your own?" The second guy comes from around one of the bushes and my heart races.

The horse huffs and starts to move away from them. I stare at her distance and try to calculate how long it would take for me to jump on her back.

"Tsk. Tsk. Tsk. Don't be like that. We just want to help you," the first one says.

"You smell like you've been claimed. Where is your alpha? Well, he's not much of an alpha if he let you out here all by yourself, now is he?"

A surge of offense on behalf of Gero and Bernhard hits me. Gero would have murdered them before they could even open their mouths in the first place. And Bernhard? He would have ripped them limb from limb.

I was stupid, wasn't I? I should have stayed where I had protection. I should have...

The first one jumps at me with a growl, and I bolt the opposite direction. My horse gets spooked and starts trotting away, leaving too much distance between us for me to catch up.

Someone grabs my leg and my head slams on the ground, stunning me for a second. A heavy body drapes over me and I kick and scream, clawing at his exposed face.

"Fuck! You're a feisty one. You reek of other males but don't worry, we'll fix that soon enough, right Chapman?"

My wrists are pinned above my head, and I turn my face to the side when he tries to kiss me.

"Fucking whore, I was trying to be nice."

"You can't be nice to whores, Aldo. You know just as well as I."

"You're right. I need to get my cock wet. Open up for me, pretty Omega." He shoves my legs apart with his knees, but I'm able to slip and knee him right in the balls, knocking him to the side.

"You bitch!" he squeals like a pig.

Rolling, I almost make it away, but the other one lands on top of me, pinning me to the ground on my stomach. My hands claw in front of me, trying to pull myself free with no use, only scraping my palms on the twigs and pebbles.

"That wasn't nice, what you did to Aldo. I'm not going to be nice to you."

He rips down my pants and I scream. It doesn't matter who knows I'm here if I'm just going to end up dead anyway.

"I love them when they scream," he says with his hot breath against the back of my head. His hand grips my hair and pulls my head back so that he can lick my cheek.

I twist my face some more and bite his tongue hard, ripping the tip off and spitting it back in his face. He howls and jerks my head back, twisting my neck to the point of pain. Why can't he just let go?

"You bitch!" comes out garbled as an elbow lands on my temple, making me see stars for a moment.

My head is pounding, and my mind is spinning, but it doesn't stop me from kicking and screaming with my eyes closed. I land a few hard kicks at his side, but we wrestle on the ground until he pins me on my side with my arm folded behind me helplessly.

My body remains tense as he pulls down my pants to my knees, locking my legs together. How is he supposed to stick it in me like this? He'll have to turn me over.

The sound of his buckle is loud in the night as I lay there, trying to distance my mind so that I don't have to fully be aware of what's about to happen to me.

At least he didn't hurt the baby. You need to protect the baby!

I can hear him stroking himself and start to wonder why it's taking so long. Surely these men were ready when they found me from the crap they spewed from their mouths.

"Give it up, Aldo. Your dick is fucked for the night."

Chapman groans, walking over to us and shoving his buddy aside. He stares down at me with fury, his hands no longer around his crotch protectively. A menacing smile crosses his face, and my leg swoops his from under him.

I can hear them both yelling as I quickly pull my pants up just far enough and shoot from the ground in a full sprint in no particular direction.

The good thing about having wide hips is that the pants stay up even when unfastened. I weave in and out of the trees, jumping over fallen branches and switching direction to make it harder for them to follow me.

I should have never made that fire. It was too obvious. I made it too easy for everyone to find me. The sad part about this escape is that I'll have to go back and see if my bag is there. I won't get far with nothing but the clothes on my back.

"She went that way! Hurry!"

"You take the left; I'll take the right."

"Come here, little pretty Omega."

Their voices waver in the dark, sounding close and then far. I'm uncertain of their direction as I continue to zig zag until I find myself in a clearing. I slide to a stop, my heart pounding out of my chest.

Oh no.

Quickly looking at every side, I choose left and run back into the thick of the woods. My legs are getting tired, and my lungs are getting winded. Turning to look over my shoulder, I run into something hard and fall back only to be caught in strong arms, turned, and have a hand slapped over my mouth.

"She went this way, I swear! There are broken branches right there."

"Aldo, you probably need a damn doctor. You're losing blood with how much is running down your face."

"Fucking bitch is going to pay!"

"Well, she can't pay if you're dead."

"Fuck!"

The crack of a branch echoes into the night. Aldo must have kicked it in his fury.

"Yeah, yeah. Come on. Once you're patched up, we can find another whore."

"Did you see her skin? She's unmarred, not one scar. A Lady. That's what I wanted a taste of. Them whores are used up cunts. It's not the same."

Chapman lets out a booming laugh and the sound of their voices fade away into the distance. But my heart doesn't relax. No. The warm body behind me breathes slowly, his chest hitting my back every so often.

He has to be male, by the sheer size of him. He feels as tall as Bernhard.

His voice comes out in a low timbre, vibrating through my body and making my eyes widen.

"What is a little omega like you doing out here, hmm? Claimed at that."

He sniffs my neck and goosebumps pebble on my skin in fear. Did I just leave two threats for this one?

"Though it is fascinating that you smell not of one male, but two. How can this be? Did they kill each other in their attempt to claim you?"

His accent is not that of any of the southern villages I've come across. I can't place it. There's a lilt to some of his vowels, but he articulates clearly.

I shake my head, not knowing what else to do. I can't speak with his hand firmly clasped over my mouth.

"If you scream, they will come back."

I nod frantically in understanding, just needing to get away from him for a breath. My paranoia is ratcheting higher and higher the longer I'm in his arms. It doesn't feel right. I don't want to touch him. I wish Bernhard was here.

"Alright, little Omega. The choice is yours. Though you're probably better off with me at the moment, don't you think?"

I nod again. Just let me go!

He chuckles under his breath and slowly removes his hand. I take in a deep inhale, trying to settle my nerves. I turn slowly to find a large, dark, cloaked figure. In the dim light of the moon, I'm unable to make out all of his features, but there's a scar under his eye that runs to the corner of his lip, twisting his smile grotesquely.

He smiles and I take a gulp, trying to figure out what I should do. I can't trust him, can I? He's another stranger out here.

"You may want to fix that," he says, looking down between my legs.

I gasp, crossing them and swiftly fastening my pants up and crossing my arms.

"Don't be scared, little Omega. If I wanted to hurt you, I would have done so already, don't you think? There's no one around us but you and me."

"I-I have to go back," I sputter, trying to make him stop talking to me. I can't think with a voice like that, one that has probably serenaded many women to fall into bed with him.

"Back?" He steps forward and I step back, closer to the clearing and illuminating his face.

His deep-set eyes are dark, inviting. A head of dark hair graces his head, curling seductively, making a woman want to touch it. His cheekbones are high, further reiterating that he's not a local. Not with those features.

The question should be, what is he doing here in the Southern Kingdom.

"I left something. Back there," I point. "I need to go back and get it."

"I see. I suppose I can accompany you in case you run into any more...trouble."

I shake my head. "No, that's alright. Thank you. I'll be fine."

I turn and run. I can't hear anyone chasing behind me, but it doesn't stop me from my mission to go find the bag I left behind. I need the money for travel. To get another horse. I need the food to last me until I make it to Harden village to deliver the letter.

I'm lost in the trees, unable to decipher the direction I came from, but the small tendrils of smoking wafting up into the night air helps me get back on track. When I make it there, my bag is nowhere to be found. Did I really think they would just leave it when it had coin?

I growl into the night and stomp my feet in frustration, slapping my fists against my head only succeeding in making it throb more.

I fall to my knees and a twig snaps. Fearfully looking over my shoulder, I see that it is the dark stranger from before. I never caught his name.

"You are a quick one. No wonder the other guys couldn't catch you. Did you find what you were looking for?"

"Do you think I would be on my knees right now if I did?" My attitude gets the better of me. My heart stops for a second, wondering if he will kill me for my mouth.

Instead, he just lets out a booming laugh. It's so annoying because even that is attractive. Despite my feminine mind telling me all this, my body doesn't want to be next to him. It responds in the exact opposite way. I scoot away slowly and get on the balls of my feet discreetly.

He raises his hands up, palm facing out in supplication. "You're skittish, to boot. I don't blame you, little Omega." The smile that graces his face is a strange one. With the distortion from his scar, I can't read his expression correctly.

My hands grip a handful of dirt right before I stand up to face him fully.

"Do you blame me, after everything that you witnessed? I don't even know your name. Why should I trust you?"

His grin widens. "Is that all it takes? The name's Severin, Severin Brooker of Orleighelbo."

The village name doesn't ring a bell whatsoever. I've never heard my grandmother or mother speak of such a place, and their travels took them far and wide.

"You'll freeze before you make it to Thatch on foot."

Thatch is the first village south of the castle. So, I'm not that far it seems. I store that information away in my mind.

Severin puts his hands down at his sides and lifts one with his palm facing up in invitation. "Why don't you let me accompany you until we reach Thatch. At least then I can rest assured you're safe. There's a tavern owned by a well-known omega. She'll be able to take you in and give you a place to rest until you get back on your feet."

It sounds perfect. Another omega would listen. They would believe what I told them because we protect our own.

I decide to take the gamble and nod my head slowly.

"That's a good little Omega. A smart choice," he coos as he drops his hand when he realizes I won't take it.

My trust only went so far. Being in his arms once was enough for a lifetime. I don't need to feel them again.

"I'll follow you to Thatch and that's it," I declare.

"Of course. Come on, then." He turns and walks away without looking back.

I follow him silently in the night, my legs still tired from the previous run. My stomach grumbles and I wrap one of my arms around it, trying to keep it calm.

Smoke billows lightly about a mile away. Is this where his camp is?

"We're almost there. Just a mile or less. Are you doing alright?"

It's kind of him to be concerned. "Yes. I'll make it." Lord, just let me make it. I need rest. Today has been too long.

I'm huffing and out of breath by the time we make it to the flickering fire. I let out a sigh of relief behind him until he steps to the side, and I see what's in front of us.

My horse. Why does he have my horse?

I open my mouth to tell him that the mare belongs to me when two chuckling men come from behind a tree, hauling more firewood.

The hairs on the back of my neck stand on end and I stop in my tracks.

"Come on, Sweetling. We have food by the fire. I heard your stomach grumbling back there. You must be famished."

He turns to walk back toward me, and I throw the dirt to his face, making him curse while I turn to run back the way we came.

Instead of a body like I anticipated, a net is thrown over me, tripping my tired legs and taking me to the ground.

Heavy footsteps walk towards me and I grip another handful of dirt and pebbles. His boot comes down on my fist, making me cry out in pain.

"Now, Sweetling. Is that any way to treat a man that was only trying to help?"

Severin, crouches down and stares at my face, the smile never leaving his, making me send up a small mental prayer.

"Little omegas go for a lot these days, did you know? Either for ransom to their alphas...or for sale to others who want to know what it feels like to have an omega beneath their feet as a slave. I heard the North is visiting. Perhaps their money conversion will be better for this deal."

"They'll find you and kill you," I threaten.

"The same way they found you? Oh wait, that's right. You're out here all by your little self. I have a feeling, no one will miss you at all, little Omega."

He stands up and whistles shrilly. "Boys, let's welcome our new guest, yeah? And please, don't touch the merchandise. We don't need her bruised up before we can even make a trade."

Grimy hands grab me by the arms and legs. I kick and flail, only to have a rough, lightly woven sack wrapped over my head and the net, shutting me out from the world.

12

BERNHARD

We made it to Treton. Word of the army from the North has already traveled this far west causing distress in the women and concern in their men.

I reared up my horse and stepped forward toward the growing crowd. Their faces were dirty, their clothes disheveled. Every village we have crossed so far looked the same. Remnants of Edelgard's prior reign. Like skeletons kept in a closet, the truth is brushed under the rug until one actually ventures out to the heart of the kingdom.

But that was a problem for another day.

I addressed them all at once. "Every capable man is called to action. We need to increase our military in preparation for what may come."

"Is it war? Are we at war, then?" someone hollers.

Looking at no one in particular, I answer simply. "If it is, wouldn't you want to be prepared? If it's not, then there's no loss, no foul."

The dust from our travels is starting to get to me, the armor we wear needing to be aired.

"Why should we send our men to help this new king? We don't even know if he's a good one."

"They say he killed our Alpha brutally. Is he going to treat us all the same once our use is done?"

"Maybe that's his plan. To send us all to our deaths so he doesn't have to deal with small village problems anymore."

That last statement ignites the crowd. Everyone begins to mumble and the noise around me grows to uncontrollable levels. We don't need an uprising while our borders need protecting.

My steed is uneasy around everyone's yelling and flailing arms. By the way things are going, I'm surprised this town didn't bring out their pitchforks to greet us. It is a good thing the heart of Treton is more of a small town rather than strictly hosting farmers.

Flashes of my life back Atford, a small fisherman's village, brings me bloody mental images of the rebellion I lived through as a child. My father led the resistance then and it cost him his life. My mother, losing her soul mate, died shortly after of a broken heart leaving me, as a young man, to fend for myself in a world I wasn't prepared for.

I am no longer that young man and I will not be my father. Let Gero rule and be the face of the kingdom. I, myself, would rather be his second from behind the curtain —his sword and executioner.

"Silence!" Philon roars.

They listen for only a moment before they start throwing

whatever they have on hand at us. One unrecognizable item hits Philon in the helmet with a loud clang. The air around us changes with his explosive fury. It gets heavy with his rage and there isn't enough time for warning when he growls, jumps off his horse and takes down the man in the crowd like a predatory beast.

Fists fly into the air and limbs are entangled as Philon gives into his bloodlust. I've never seen him like this. He's always been so subdued beside Raban and his attitude. Then again, our times in the dungeons never allowed us to do much.

He reminds me so much of Gero and the changes I've seen in him since our uprising. Have we all been affected somehow and just didn't know it? *Have I been affected?*

The crowd grows wider and wider, everyone stepping away from the sight before them. Blood sprays and bones audibly crack. I slowly get off my horse, pet the side of his neck and walk toward the brawl letting it play out how it must.

By the time I make it, Philon's fists are sliding off the other man's face covered in glistening red, the impact sounding more like wet slaps. Philon stops. He's heaving, grabbing his temples and growling in frustration as he brings himself back to his feet and spits out a wad of blood from his own mouth right at the crowd.

You can take the man out of the prison, but you can't take the prisoner out of the man.

Crossing my arms, I keep a safe distance away from the beast and glare at the crowd that has finally fallen into silence. Philon's rage slowly recedes, but not enough for the crowd to feel comfortable after the savagery they witnessed.

"Let him be an example to you all here. The King's military is conscripting. It starts *now*. Every able-bodied man *will* join. Be ready to leave your families in the next three hours."

"Fuck that," Philon interrupts with a snarl. "Be ready in two hours. I'm tired of this fucking place."

I nod while not taking my eyes off the crowd. "You heard the man, move!"

Some of the men stumble over each other in a race to get to their homes and pack their things. The women have their hands over their mouths, looking at us all with abject horror while trying to turn their faces away from the dead man on the ground.

They can keep their opinions. If war comes to our doorsteps, there will be more death than they can handle. At least with their men joining our numbers, we would have a fighting chance.

My mother's haunting cries float into my mind.

"I can't live without you. Not like this. There's nothing left for me in this life," my mother sobs on her knees. *Suddenly, she throws her head back and screams into the sky. "Why? Why did you take him from me?"*

"I'm so sorry, Mother," I whisper under my breath from the doorway. *"You still have me..."*

I shake my head to dislodge the memories. My chest aches from the lingering emotions of my childhood as I watched her slowly wither away from our home. Each day she cursed the sky. Each day she asked why.

My hard glare at the women of this town turn into a sympathetic one, but I voice nothing. Nothing can be said to assuage what they are feeling right now. This is the way of things, the way of life.

Philon rolls his shoulder from where he still stands, turns his head to look at me a moment before walking back to his horse with a deathly swagger. I do the same. Everything that needs to be said has been.

Getting back on my horse, I pull the reins away from the heart of Treton. As our mounts trot away, parting the people and moving down the cobbled roads, an air of resignation follows us. The farther we head out in the Southern Kingdom, the more chances we have of running into situations like these.

Are we to always make an example of someone?

"These wretched bastards are lucky I only stopped at him. I wasn't meant to be this person, some sort of royal whatnot. I'm just a simple butcher," Philon growls.

I scoff and stare at a blood soaked Philon. "A butcher, eh? What is a simple butcher doing in the royal dungeons?"

He smiles with crimson coated teeth right before he lets out a bellowing laugh like a lunatic, refusing to answer my question. I shake my head and let him keep his secrets. After all, we all have our own. Right now, I just need a drink. We've successfully ridden through six villages and it was time for a well-deserved break. The men needed it.

"We stop for the night and make camp on the outskirts of Treton," I announce. "You men are welcome to visit the taverns but keep your wits about you in case we need to move quickly."

By the time we put up our tents, the sun has fallen from the sky to the west, casting long shadows across the land. Dark figures connected to our feet, exaggerating the sheer size of our group.

"Bernhard, I'm going to one of the taverns I saw on the

way in. Do you want to join me?" Benedict calls out. He's one of the soldiers that pledged loyalty to Gero after his omega begged him to.

"Yeah. That sounds good. Give me a minute." I tuck my items and provisions away, deep inside my tent. Some of the men have volunteered to stay behind and keep watch while we make our way into the village in rotation.

Taking off my armor, I lay that in front and roll my neck, stretching my arms overhead. I never thought I would see my freedom under Edelgard's rule. Pardons were almost unheard of. I had resigned my fate to the dungeons with Gero by my side.

Gero.

Making my way toward the other men, there are about seven of us in total. A good number to watch each other's backs in a town that does not favor us. Benedict slaps the back of my shoulder and I tilt my head to the other men in greeting. With smiles, we head back on the cobbled roads of the town on foot.

I wonder how Gero is faring back at the castle. He has Idalia to keep him warm and sane. Despite his attitude of not needing anyone, it's a lie. I don't know his story, but there is a void within him. A darkness he keeps at bay while showing the world a different face. He may think I don't know, but I do. Darkness knows darkness, and he is one of the blackest ones I've come across forged by whatever experience he went through before the dungeons.

Women skirt around us, choosing a different path once we walk by too closely. I inwardly scoff. It was the same back in the village of Atford. The son of the leader of the rebellion, cursed by his bloodline.

Ignoring them, we reach a wooden building with clean windows. One thing can be said about this place. Their people walk around disheveled while their buildings look well kept. It was a fact I put away in the back of my mind.

One of the men pushes the door open to find a dark and dim atmosphere. Wooden pillars and tables fill the room. A bar sits at the far back with stools that have seen better days. The benches that sit beside the tables are more intact and most of the patrons are staring at us with hidden disdain.

The music stops upon our entering, but suddenly starts again to bring the mood back to what it once was.

"Let's drink this day away and celebrate the fact that we've successfully collected a good number of men," one of the guys says. Hugh, I think his name was. He was collected from the first time I set out.

"Here, here to that."

We seat ourselves at the bar. Benedict hails down the barkeeper, ordering all of us a mug of ale. The liquid splashes on the counter as the barkeep brings out our drinks. The smell reminds me of the meetings my father held back in my hometown. Rooms hidden beneath the village in tunnels and caverns.

The local authorities knew nothing about it, many of them meeting in the middle of the night and sometimes broad daylight at odd hours. I was young, stupid, and looked up to my father. I would sneak into the meetings where I could, learning all their strategies and plans.

It wasn't something a fisherman's boy should know.

Like what a woman's moan feels like when the rebellion celebrated their small victories.

A feminine screech pulls me from my thoughts, and I

look over my shoulder to find one of the barmaids in a patron's lap, laughing giddily.

Idalia would have slit his throat if he tried that with her. I take a swig of my drink and smile, thinking about how I would find her upon my return.

Gero never did fuck her enough. Or maybe he held back for me.

My face flushes at the notion and I hide it behind another swig of ale.

"Are you looking for a good time tonight, men?"

"Why is a beautiful woman like you asking questions like that?" Hugh asks back.

The female leans in, giving us all a good look at her cleavage spilling out as she traces her finger along his jaw.

"I fancy a man that can handle a girthy sword in his hands."

Hugh gets to his feet immediately, knocking his stool down with a loud crash, diverting everyone's attention to us as he throws her over his shoulder and walks out the front door, slapping her on the ass.

Her squeals can be heard fading away the farther they get.

"Betas are loose, am I right, men?" Benedict chuckles.

"If they are, I'm going to need one to empty my sac before we head out," one of the other guys pipes in.

"What about you, Bernhard?"

I continue to drink my ale, finishing my cup. "The only thing about me is I gotta take a piss."

Getting up, I give them all a glare. "Stay out of trouble until I get back."

"Yes sir!" A few of them mock salute as they stare at some of the other betas and a few shy gammas looking their way.

I make my way around the tables, checking the layout and seeing if there's a back door to the place. No sense in pissing in front of a nicely cleaned building. The pitchforks would really come out then.

The place is busy, full of voices and different conversations, even some light moans. One particular conversation float to my ear.

"Are you okay, dear?" an older woman asks.

"Y-Yes. I just..."

The younger female's voice is shaken.

"Say no more. Here's some food and I'll be back with some coin. I knew that man was no good since his father first brought him in here."

"I'm so sorry..."

"Why are you sorry? He's the one that beat you. Get that silly notion out of your head, girl. You're going to need your wits about you once you leave."

"I'm leaving?"

"Yes. There is another tavern in the Town of Thatch, run by a very sweet omega and her alpha. They will take you in and help you get back on your feet. It's far enough from that bastard husband of yours that you'll be safe." She calls for, who I assume to be, her husband and tells him to ready his horse.

It's not my problem, I tell myself as I continue to walk toward the back exit and make my way into the fresh air.

There are barrels and sacks of supplies back here but not much else. Not wanting to taint the tavern owner's supplies, I walk further out and around the corner.

Hugh must have had the same idea as he continues to pound into the beta with his hand over her mouth to prevent her cries from escaping. My thoughts float to Idalia and her little spitfire attitude, making my dick semi-erect.

Groaning under my breath, I turn toward the corner of the building, unfasten my pants and let my piss flow, sending waves of pleasure up my spine. Gritting my teeth until the last ounce is released, I sigh, shake my cock, and tuck myself back in.

It's going to be a long recruitment by the time we make it to the end of the West Territories, to the south, and then back up to the castle in Dodbrid. Gero better be fucking our girl senseless until then, keeping her wet and ready for me.

My mouth waters at the thought of what his dick would taste like in my mouth covered in her scent.

EPILOGUE

IDALIA

My body is rocking as if I'm on something moving. The air around me is warming, telling me I'm under the heat of the sun. It's daylight. Blinking my eyes a few times, I'm confused at the flickering of light through fabric until I fully come to.

I'm in the back of a cart of some sort, shoulders against boxes and other items, with a bag still strapped over my head. Light desperately tries to filter through the loose weave of the potato sack, casting shadows every time we pass by an overgrowth of trees and branches. My hands are tied behind my back uncomfortably. My mouth is stuffed with dirty cloth, making it dry and wanting to vomit at the same time.

The sound of men chattering away and letting out stupid laughs to the left helps me to remember what happened to put me in this predicament.

Severin.

He played me like an instrument, making me put my guard down with his charm to bring me back to his camp only to find that he's been working with the other two all along. The two that tried to rape me and stole my bag of supplies.

And my horse. Damnit, he has my horse!

"So, what did he give ya for coming all the way down here?" Idiot number one says. They must be sitting at the front of the cart. I wonder if my mare is strapped to it.

"You're mistaken, my friend. I've always been down here," Severin replies in his lilt.

"Yeah? You from the coast or somethin'?" idiot number two pipes in.

"Something," he chuckles, but doesn't expand.

In a previous life, my mother and grandmother have done trade with pirates before when we ventured south or toward the inlet towns. Fisherman towns were wary of them, but rumors of a rebellion starting changed their feelings on that. They needed weapons; they needed items that would help them win.

As a young girl, I remember the day my grandmother told us that we were never to trade in places like Atford or Shoney again. I was too young to wonder or question why.

"Got a big secret, do ya?" idiot number one breaks the silence.

"Don't we all?"

Is Severin a pirate? That would explain why his accent sounds so mixed. Maybe he was part of the rebellion. I could have sworn Edelgard quelled that during his rise to power after his father passed.

I continue to ponder the possibilities of where he's from

and where we're going while slowly pushing out the disgusting rag from my mouth with my tongue. The men continue to banter back and forth at the front of the cart, but I drown it out. My jaw begins to ache by the time it fully dislodges. Pulling in air through my nose, I flex my jaw and fully close my mouth. I wonder how long I've been out. With my tongue, I try to rewet the inside by moving the muscle around. It's salty and something else, inducing my gag reflex but I try to hold it back. My head is still in a bag after all.

The rocking of the cart doesn't help my nausea as I shut my eyes and try to breathe in slowly to calm my stomach. I didn't get to eat much since my run and my body has probably burned up all that was in there by now.

We continue to ride on for what feels like an hour before my bladder screams from the inside and I'm scissoring my legs to prevent myself from pissing all over the only pair of clothes I brought with me.

My thoughts drift to Bernhard and I send another silent prayer up for him to find me somehow or at least tell Gero so that he may send men out to find me. I should have stayed.

The cart abruptly stops, rolling me hard against a wooden crate. I bite my lip to stop a groan from escaping but it's too late.

The cart jolts from someone jumping off and the sound of footsteps come my way.

"Hey Sweetling, I hope you enjoyed the ride. You were nice and quiet back here like a good little omega."

Two hands grip me roughly and I get tossed onto a shoulder with an oomph. I really scissor my legs then and Severin chuckles as he tosses me down onto my feet, making me stumble backward. His hands are quick as they catch me and jerk the bag off my head.

"Woah, steady now. I got you. I just wanted to give you time to relieve yourself."

Good. And bad. Who's going to help me, him? I refuse to let him touch me again. My body shivers from the thought and his smile widens.

"I'll be glad to have the other guys assist you, but I can't guarantee they won't assist themselves with anything else."

I glare at him for a long moment, my bladder about to erupt right here. Gritting my teeth inside my mouth, I nod my head without taking my eyes off him.

"Ah, good choice. I knew you were a smart little omega. Now, turn around and I'll help you unfasten your pants," he coos seductively, and I want to bite his face off.

Instead, I do as I'm told. His hands slowly roam to the front of me, his fingers moving slow. A growl does escape me then, making him laugh.

My pants are shoved down to my ankles and he forces me to squat with his grip on my tied hands and his other against my back, pushing me forward.

My mind shuts out the embarrassment, the only thing running through it are promises of retribution when I escape.

Something wet rubs against my pussy lips and I gasp at the coldness.

"Shh. Let me wash you. Omega's like to be taken care of, don't they?"

"I can take care of her once you're done," idiot number one says, and I tremble for a second. I'm sure he would love to.

Severin brings me to my feet and refastens my pants with the same slow speed he used when unfastening.

"That's alright, Chapman. I think I got this. Seems the ladies tend to prefer my soft touches, you see."

"Pfft. She's an omega. She'll take it the way she gets it."

I'm going to kill him first when I get out of here.

Severin pets my arms and I flinch away with disgust. He ignores it, petting me more firmly as if to calm a stray animal that's been caught in a cage.

"You've got a lot to learn Beta. Omegas are complicated little things."

Without warning, I'm lifted and tossed onto Severin's shoulder once more, my head behind him glaring at Chapman who glares right back.

"Omegas are a dime a dozen. What do I care about their complications? Fuck 'em. That's all they need to be happy."

"Tsk, tsk, tsk," Severin replies as he unceremoniously dumps me into the back of the cart with a crash, slamming my back onto who knows what, sending pain up my spine and knocking the wind out of me.

"You'll learn," he says as he walks away toward the front.

Chapman sneers at me with his arms crossed. I feel the same way about you, ya prick.

"This one will get us good trade up North, I guarantee it."

Chapman's sneer deepens and morphs into a menacing smile as he turns and joins in with Severin.

The North? What does he mean North? He can't mean what I think he means...

"So that's the plan, is it? You didn't tell us that was where we were going," Aldo says, his tongue still giving him trouble.

"Who said I needed to tell you guys? You were only paid to go as far as Knutstowy."

"You're a real rat bastard."

"We are one and the same. It doesn't matter. You guys will be leaving us in about ten miles. Take your gold and silver, buy your whores, and forget this all happened. Are we clear?"

Severin talks and acts like an alpha but I can't read his emotions or get a good feel for him. He could be a delta for all I know.

If that's the case, who's the alpha he's working under? Is that who I am to be delivered to? What is the point of my capture? I'm just one omega among a million others. Gero hasn't left the castle since the uprising. No one would recognize the scent of the new king.

My lashes flutter as I begin to drift to sleep from the slow rocking of the cart. I don't fight it, telling myself I might as well get some rest for whatever fight I may have later when we make our stop in the next town.

BOOM!

Suddenly, I'm tossed out of the cart and the sound of shattering wood gets dulled by the ringing in my ear.

My face throbs in pain from the impact against a rock on the ground, stunning me for a moment. I rock my body left and right, trying to readjust my position but with my hands still tied behind my back, it's difficult.

When I'm finally able to get onto my knees, I turn my face to cough and sputter from the dust still flying around us. What was that? What would be strong enough to do such a thing?

My body aches and my ears still ring, switching from one ear to another and back again.

"Fucking hell."

"Looks like we lost Aldo."

"Shit—"

Chapman gurgles on something before he could even finish his sentence. I know that sound well. My eyes widen as I try to scoot backward on my butt, looking for somewhere I can hide behind.

"Guess, I'll be keeping your payment guys. It's the way of business after all, you understand. Me and my little Omega have a long journey ahead of us."

The sound of Severin flicking the blood off his blade sends a chill down my spine. For all of his smiles and charms, I never saw this coming. Was this his plan all along? Why destroy the whole cart? How are we getting to wherever it is he needs to get to?

"Damn, you didn't have to hit us that hard, you know? You ruined my best set of clothes," he says nonchalantly. Is he talking to me?

I wiggle until I get myself back onto my feet and run as stealthy as I can toward the cover of trees nearby right off the dirt road we've been traveling on.

"You were taking too long, and I got tired of waiting. Leave their bodies here for the crows. Where's the merchandise?"

I make it past a few trees until I find the biggest one to hide behind, leaning my back against it and trying to calm my racing heart.

"Now, now. You know how this goes. I need to see the money first before you can see the merchandise."

"You're a damn liar and a thief. I don't think you even have what you promised."

"A ship is an expensive item. Money is important in any transaction. You show me yours and I'll go and find mine and bring her back."

The sound of coins being tossed on the ground echoes in the silence.

"That wasn't so hard, was it?"

"Ahhh!" The stranger's cries of agony are quickly cut short by the sound of bones crunching and a blade cutting through the air.

I've been silently biting my lip, rubbing the stupid rope against the bark of the tree, hoping to break the strands as fast as I can before I make another run for it. Just my luck, the rope gets caught in the stub of a broken branch, making me jerk my arms until there's a loud snap, exposing my position.

I gasp and run without looking back. My legs have rested enough to not feel as achy as the first night. Dodging low hung branches and jumping over large stones, I weave in and out unsure of my direction, led purely on survival instinct.

My horse, if strapped to the front of the cart, is probably dead by now. I've given up hope on that. I need to find a cave; I need to find somewhere I can hide!

Bracing myself to jump over the fallen log that's coming up, I take a deep breath and leap. Thank goodness for pants. Halfway into the air, something hard hits me from the side, taking us both to ground, scraping my right side against the gravel and twigs.

Hissing, I roll over and groan, trying to pull my arms from their bondage. I know I cut through at least halfway, there's leeway in my movements now. If I can just use my strength, I may be able to break it the rest of the way!

His smell hits my nostrils and I grimace.

"You do give me a run for my money, Sweetling." He licks the sweat from the side of my face, and I flinch. "I may have to reconsider giving you up. You're much too fun to be around."

Severin stands up and pulls me with him by the arm. I refuse to look at him. Refuse to give him the satisfaction of surrender. I'm not going to give up. I'm going to escape and kill him if it's the last thing I do.

"That murderous look in your eye makes my cock hard. Unless you want me to do something about it, I suggest you play nice."

Visibly swallowing, I blink a few times and school my features.

"That's a good little Omega. Now come along, it was a good thing the impact hit our cart on the side and not the front. Your mare awaits us.

"Where are you taking me? What do you want with me?"

Severin chuckles as we walk back in the direction of the shattered cart. I still don't know what hit us.

"Don't you know? Your father sent me to find you."

COMING SOON...

If you get your kicks in a magical manner, order toys from websites like bad dragon, and prefer your monsters *in* your bed instead of *under* them, then Y. D. is your girl.

Writing everything from spicy dark fantasy to fluffier-than-a-cool-marshmallow romance, Y.D. La Mar has her fingers in all sorts of man-meat pie, and the sky is the limit. Somehow, this magical mistress manages to balance her spicy author life with her responsibilities as a mom, a wife, and a resident of Sin City—*oh, irony, you've felled me.*

When the world is full of black-and-white, Y.D. plays in the grey zones, spending her time creating new ways to shock and awe her editor, as well as her readers.

Follow Me!

WANT UPDATES AND SNEAK PEEKS?

Sign up for my newsletter!

ALSO BY YD LA MAR

STREET ARRHYTHMIA TRILOGY

The Scent of Jasmine

For The Love of Import & Blood

To The Beat of The Streets

Spinoff

Arachnophilia

REVERSE HAREM

Warring Suns

SCI FI

The Essence of Esme

PARANORMAL

The Hunger of Thieves

Heart of The Reaper

Heart of the Reaper: Tales from the Underworld

Soul of The Reaper

Fate of The Reaper

Bury Me Alive

Lead Me Through The Fire

PSYCHOLOGICAL THRILLER

The Truth Enslaved

CONTEMPORARY

The Formation of Us

The Conception of Us

The Revelation of Us

The House of Eden (cowrite)

When the Bloom Burns (cowrite)

OMEGAVERSE

Gero

Bernhard

Severin

DYSTOPIAN/POST APOCALYPTIC

We Are the Fallen

MONSTER SHORT STORIES

Sinful Attraction

The Sky Below

Maeonia

Between Heaven and Earth

Fantasies Inflamed

Her 13th Hour

Ignus Fatuus

ANTHOLOGIES

Used and Bound

Captured by Darkness

Until the End

After the Rain

Into The Woods

A Foster Fling

Bound by Monsters

Once Upon a Nightmare

Monsters in Love: Lost in the Dark

Monsters in Love: Lost in the Forest

Monsters in Love: Monstrous Ever After

Monsters in Love: Lost in the Deeps

Monsters in Love: Aloha Nui Loa

Pollinators

The Red Key Club: Valentines Day Edition

The Red Key Club: Halloween Edition

Creepy Court

Crimson Vendetta

For the Love of Villains

SHARED WORLDS

Inferno World

Games of the Underworld

Rise of the Dreads

Monsters Ball

Rescue Me: A Hero Romance Collection